WINDFALL NIGHTS

WILLIAM CLAYPOOL

iUniverse, Inc.
Bloomington

iUniverse books may be ordered through booksellers or by contacting:

iUniverse
1663 Liberty Drive
Bloomington, IN 47403
www.iuniverse.com
1-800-Authors (1-800-288-4677)

Because of the dynamic nature of the Internet, any web addresses or links contained in
this book may have changed since publication and may no longer be valid. The views
expressed in this work are solely those of the author and do not necessarily reflect the
views of the publisher, and the publisher hereby disclaims any responsibility for them.

ISBN: 978-1-4620-0470-6 (sc)
ISBN: 978-1-4620-0471-3 (hc)
ISBN: 978-1-4620-0472-0 (ebook)

Printed in the United States of America

Library of Congress Control Number: 2011903925

iUniverse rev. date: 04/21/2011

To Cissy

Thank you for encouraging me to see this (and many other more important items) through to the end.

NOTE

Two Rivulets side by side,
Two blended, parallel, strolling tides,
Companions, travelers, gossiping as they journey.

For the Eternal Ocean bound,
These ripples, passing surges, streams of Death and Life,
Object and Subject hurrying, whirling by,
The Real and Ideal,
Alternate ebb and flow the Days and Nights,
(Strands of a Trio twining, Present, Future, Past.)

Walt Whitman ("The Poet") — 1876

CHAPTER 1

Anna lay sleeping in our stateroom when I left before dawn. She was distant from me when we went to bed, and she had a restless night. She had her memories to work through, as I had mine. In one form or another, Thomas had been in our lives for nearly forty years, and although I might have tried to forget him, it doesn't always work that way. Anna would not try to forget. She would love to freeze every moment and postpone every good-bye, but I wasn't that strong. I escape by denial, and with this denial sleep comes easily. After my breakfast I found a deck lounge chair and managed to nod off above the deep, muffled vibrations of the massive engines six decks below.

Our cruise ship turned from the South China Sea at daybreak to begin the four-hour trip up the Saigon River. My lounge chair was fully shaded on the afterdeck when I first climbed on. Now the rising tropical sun was full on my lower legs, and they were stinging from its intensity. It was barely past nine.

Forty years ago, we could not have imagined a trip to this place. The trip was my gift to Anna, although truthfully, it was her idea. Examining the old scars of memory is always risky and not my particular talent. Even happy recollections are dappled with the reality that their time is gone.

1

The previous evening I had received an e-mail announcing an upcoming college reunion. It wouldn't merit a second thought were it not for the coincidence of receiving it here, traveling to Saigon. Those last college days were really not forgotten, and over time, the good had come to overshadow the bad. But no matter how bright the light, there are shadows somewhere. None of the bad was really my tragedy, if it was a tragedy at all. But I was just close enough to be wounded by it. I simply watched it all and came to wonder whether any power on earth could have changed it. For years, I lived with the guilt that perhaps I should have tried harder. But Thomas never fully let me in, and I never really had the chance. It was just so strange to watch him and then to lose him, not all at once but just a little at a time. Then he was completely gone.

I was still alone on the afterdeck, but I knew it would not last. This floating five-star hotel was a remarkable purchase from which to watch the river already bustling with commercial traffic, and my fellow pampered guests would soon come to join me. Cargo barges muscled in the channel with the rusted mini-freighters below the flags of every Asian country. Hard goods, currency makers for their vibrant economy, had been in full march since first light. The flag most flown was the red banner with the central yellow star. Real ships flew big flags, and shallow-draft freighters hoisted smaller flags, but they almost all sailed under the Vietnamese flag. The banner had spread from the Vietminh to the Northern Communists and to all of the country after the fall. That flag was now everywhere on this wide river.

For most, it must be a symbol of pride for the only country they knew. For others of a certain age it must be like a rape victim who gave birth and raised and loved her child while hating the father. It was another reason not to dwell on old memories.

I walked to the rail for a wider view. I had been joined by two couples, but they kept to themselves. There were few distractions from my little world to behold the magic beyond. They say that the human eye can see eight million colors, and as I looked out to the vivid forested kingdom surrounding the river, it seemed certain that most of those must be hues of green. There were no defoliated or bomb-cratered moonscapes here like there were up-country many years back. Mixed with the green in the distance were villages growing to towns, and occasional factories. Construction cranes were numerous on the horizon in all directions. Occasionally we would pass small fishing boats with fathers and sons creeping close to shore out of the channel. Everywhere was life and energy and building and growth. It had not been so forty years ago.

Engrossed with the scene, I did not immediately notice Anna next to me on the rail until she took my arm. I turned to her, and she smiled and kissed me on the cheek.

"How did you sleep?" I asked.

She shrugged her shoulders and said, "Not bad," with neither conviction nor honesty. "How are you feeling?"

"I'm okay. I'm amazed at this country all over again." I gestured out beyond the river.

She nodded but said nothing as we watched the river pass below the rail.

Forty years ago we, as a country, were somewhere in the five stages of dealing with our inevitable dying and death in the South. Instead of starting with denial and working up to acceptance, we muddled along with slogans designed to appease the US Congress. We started this as a training and education mission. After the Tonkin Resolution, we ratcheted it up a notch or two to pacification. Before and then certainly after Tet, we got mad and flipped the dial to full-blown eradication—with certain civil limits for political reasons. Body counts were the new metric, but try as we might, within those proper constraints, we couldn't kill them all. Failing that, we sacked Westmoreland and then tried, perhaps a bit late, to wage the hearts-

and-minds approach. Then, sensing complete disaster, Nixon put up the white flag and called it "Vietnamization"; in time, Congress followed suit and pulled the plug on supplies and equipment. At that point, the North Vietnamese Army and Charlie said, "Let's start the party."

The party was a nightmare for our former friends. The tree of this single nation, if not the tree of liberty, was indeed amply refreshed with the blood of the patriots. The martyrs of Vietnam, both North and South, must be resting somewhat easier these days as some prosperity and stability had returned after a long absence.

"It's really hot out here," said Anna. "Can I get you something to drink?"

"Sure. I'll have whatever you're drinking."

She patted me on the arm and went through the glass doors to the bar.

Watching her go, I remembered the reunion notice. The reunion wasn't one of the big ones, not a five or a zero to make it "significant." It's a matter of convenience to reflect on the passage of time at wide and predicable intervals, but I find it more convenient not to think about it at all. I've never been to a reunion—high school, college, or graduate school. I didn't like most of the people then, and I had no interest in giving them five- and ten-year updates. But the notice served as a mnemonic to me (or in this country can I still consider it an "aide memoire"?). Thomas never finished school; the reunion wasn't for him.

I did finish, and it was a struggle for me. I guess my heart was only partially in it for much of the time. My mother died when I was nineteen after a long, terrible, ugly siege against her cancer. But before she went, she forced me into a deathbed promise to finish what I started. I made the promise, but I didn't start it. She did. I didn't want to leave home when she was so sick, but she pushed me out. She had been a schoolteacher and prized learning more than anything other than family, so I had to go. I was her only child, and she invested all she had left in me. When I went to school, she knew that she was going to die and to die soon. I thought it a burden to carry so much love, and it was a cruel separation.

After she died, Dad struggled for a time to keep loving life and tried briefly to get through his grief, but then he surrendered. He married a woman named Barbara. He never loved her like Mom and spent the rest of his life looking backward. They eventually had two daughters, and he was as attentive to them as he was neglectful of her and me. We grew to like and tolerate each other as distant friends, not as father and son. For better or worse, we were friends who tolerated long absences, spoke infrequently, and had no dependence on one another.

Anna returned with orange juice for both of us. She had gone to our cabin and found a hat to fight the sun. She was fascinated with the people on the river. She made eye contact with the fishermen with their children venturing near the channel, and when she did she would wave. She called out greetings in Vietnamese until she realized that they couldn't hear her.

The landscape palette was becoming less natural and more man-made. There was more iron in the waterway as we came up on anchorage after anchorage for the river traffic coming into the city. There were more clearings in the jungle, more commercial buildings, and more small boat traffic around us. The vitality of the country was infectious, even to the ship, as my fellow passengers, now invading the deck in force, spoke excitedly in half a dozen languages. Anna seemed to enjoy the growing crowd.

When an elderly Vietnamese couple we had seen at a dining table the previous evening came near us, Anna spoke to them in Vietnamese. They responded, and she smiled at me.

"They want to know if it's our first time in Vietnam. They live in LA, and it's their first time back since 1976. They were boat people, and they lost both of their children trying to get out. He runs a chain of specialty grocery stores now."

She spoke again in bursts of Vietnamese phrases that sounded to my ear only slightly slower than their own. They seemed impressed with what she told them. They smiled to her again and then went to the other side of the deck where the old man was particularly interested in pointing something out to his wife.

"I'll be right back," said Anna. "I want to hear a little of his commentary." Then she drifted over to their side of the deck.

While it was during my first time "in-country" that I last saw Thomas, it was not my last trip. I did my job too well the first time. They sent me back … again and again. I saw the whole country with a bit of Cambodia thrown in as a bonus. I didn't mind it—except for the war. I was never a soldier. I was just a writer and an industry whistle-blower. I worked for a small technical engineering magazine at the time. George, my editor, was very big on design and materials testing, and he felt that neither of them was ever done sufficiently for the equipment the soldiers used. I felt like a Judas to the soldiers, not for what I was doing, but for what I purported to be. The more I knew the soldiers, the more I liked them and the less I liked myself. They were trying to improve their equipment, but my editors just wanted dirt and more dirt. It wasn't hard to find; it's never hard to find in a war. My angle was always technical—something failing under fire, jamming, or never working at all. Everything from helmet straps to artillery shells was fair game. They figured that if my story didn't work well in print, they could sell it directly to the equipment manufacturer and the "hush money" would at least cover my expenses. It was a sound business plan, although they never needed to walk the extortion route with my pieces. At the time, anything negative written about the war sold. Talent was nice, but timing was everything.

George would love to compliment me in the only way he could. He would usually rush up and place his hand on my shoulder and say, "Julian, you write like a moron, but no one finds more crap than you. Keep it up and don't worry—we can fix the writing." Then he would dash off. Within a few months I hated my job, but the pay was good and I stayed at it for longer than I would have guessed.

I looked around the deck. Anna was within earshot, speaking French to another very old couple. She looked happy to be speaking with them, so I went back to my sightseeing.

Barges at anchorage were off-loading supplies to smaller boats as we came to the outskirts of Saigon. Flat boats with long-shaft outboards came and went on the channel, provisioning the small freighters with fresh fruit, vegetables, chickens, and whatever else one could carry and the other could afford. Police and government patrol craft loitered on the channel margins. The green uniforms of their soldiers made me uneasy even after all this time. That seemed absurd. I had never been in combat there. I was near it, but it never came to me. But those uniforms still frightened me.

I tried to connect with Thomas on each trip back but only managed to see him that first time there. He had his job, and I had mine. We corresponded for a time, but it didn't stick. We both blamed the logistics initially, but we each just drifted along with our own worlds. We last connected with a birthday card. It was okay, though. It was mutual. We were both well-practiced at running alone.

Anna returned to my side as the ship's crew prepared to dock.

"Julian, do you ever wonder how different life might be if only a few events went the other way?"

She had asked me this question many times before. She obviously was wondering about a specific event that morning.

"Anna, I don't think about it that way. On the highway of life, it's only a one-way street, no matter what route you take."

"It may be only a one-way street, love, but it's been no highway for us. It's been a bumpy road with a lot of corners, and we've had to make decisions at each one of them."

I let a moment pass watching the docking procedure. "I don't like looking back very much. It's not worth the pain."

She paused and then said, "Well, I can't help it."

We sat quietly watching as our captain delicately maneuvered the giant ship sideways along the cement pier. The only noteworthy event of the landing was the dockside display of a dozen beautiful young women who held a banner that said "Welcome to Vietnam." Given the commercial firepower of this cruise ship, that was good business, and this country was all about business. Ho Chi Minh City was fading, and Saigon was what the city was starting to be called again. Despite politics, Saigon was a far better brand name.

"Come on," she said, becoming bored with the ship's landing. "It's too hot out here. Let's go back to the cabin." She took my hand and led me back to our stateroom where she turned the fan higher and just stood in front of the air conditioner for a few minutes. Refreshed, she walked over to the veranda and opened the door.

As we sat in still waters next to the quay, it was all starting to settle in. Anna knew what I was feeling, and she was dealing with her own memories. I thought of the other trips here. Most were in the delta about two hours south by a normal drive, although it usually took longer then. It was an amazing part of an incredible country that somehow teemed with life and quick death at the same time. It was also part Eden and was now redesigned for tourists in a way that would make Disney happy. But I wasn't thinking of going back. I wasn't thinking of much besides my last visit with Thomas and then the time before and then the time after.

She came to me sitting on the bed and squeezed my arm again.

"Did you remember that today is the date of Margery's death?"

I hesitated for a moment. "Yes. I remembered."

"It's hard to believe," she said. "I still miss her."

"I do too."

Outside the veranda, we saw that the crew had secured all the lines and maneuvered the gangway to the dock. The engines shut down, and the city noises seemed closer on the lower deck with the veranda door open.

"You were like a son to her, Julian."

"Well, a good friend, anyway."

"No, you were the best son a mother could have."

I let the comment linger for a moment and then hugged her and simply said, "Thanks."

"You remember that we're meeting my friend Kim Mai for dinner, right?"

I nodded.

"Good. Would you mind if I went up to the salon? There's a scarf I wanted to buy for tonight, and the ship's gift shops close at noon today."

"Sure, go ahead, but wouldn't it make more sense to go into town and pick up something there?"

She smiled at me and said, "Julian, I've had my eye on this scarf since Hong Kong." She kissed me on the cheek and walked to the door. "Oh, and if they can fit me in, I may get my nails done before we go out, okay?"

"Fine. We'll go ashore about noon then?"

"Yes, can you wait that long?"

"I've waited almost forty years."

She smiled at me again as she left.

The anniversary date of Margery's death, the reunion announcement, and the arrival in Saigon—it was a strange coincidence for these to collide on the same morning. This was an intersection of events that should not be—or perhaps it should.

Some of my evangelical friends believe there is no such thing as a coincidence with a loving God. He runs all facets of the universe, and we can relax with Him in charge. It's all arranged for us, like a giant complex psychology experiment with God adjusting all the rewards and punishments. All we have to do is deal with it. The other side says it's random and it just happens. As their theory goes, as much as God loves us, He just doesn't want to interfere.

CHAPTER 2

Thomas's mother, Margery, was responsible for our first meeting in Vietnam. We had corresponded and spoken frequently since Thomas left. She knew all about my life since college. At the time, I confided more in her than in my fiancée. I lived in New York and then Washington, but even though she was still in Indiana, there was no real distance between us. I wrote her that I was going "in-country." She was determined that I would see Thomas again, which meant it would happen.

George gave me the assignment only about three weeks before I was to travel. The assignment was to be the first of a small series on mess kit items failing in the field. It was a low-tech angle—rusting spoons, failing handles on heating plates, leaking canteen caps—but one that immediately got the attention of procurement people. Management was confident that I could find something wrong with the soldiers' mess kits, and they thought the resulting story would be worth the expense of my airfare and a good hotel.

After coming into Saigon, still half scrambled from jet lag, I found my way from the airport to the Rex Hotel. It was far above my station, but my editor thought that I could use the accommodations to induce some field-grade officers to allege that their supplies were substandard and hurt soldiers in the field. Since none of their

11

remarks would be directly attributable (a real coward's defense), it only took about four shots of whiskey on average to get to what my editor called the "truth." Colleagues back in Washington would then take the story to the procurement bureaucrats at the Pentagon, who would either defend their actions or refer the investigators to the contractors. After the second day and the sixth interview, I had my story.

Margery said that Thomas would meet me the next day. She knew the name of my hotel, but the arrangement was for me to meet him in the small park in front of the cathedral across from the main post office. The rendezvous point was just a few blocks away from my hotel. It was Sunday and early. The usual crushing flow of bicycles, motorbikes, cars, and trucks had not yet developed. On my walk over there, I saw that the shops oozed America. American soft drinks, candies, household goods, and cigarettes were conspicuous in all the kiosks.

The landmark church was easy to find. Large, red-brick, and across from the post office, the Catholic basilica was a wonderful vestige of the colonial French. Each brick came from France, and at the time, they must have thought it to be an enormous works project. What a difference a hundred years makes. They would not have been able to comprehend the real construction marvels of Vietnam a hundred years later, such as the aviation infrastructure of Da Nang or the shipping and logistics facilities at Cam Ranh Bay.

When I arrived at the church, Mass was just letting out and people were milling in the little church park in front of the main door. This small green peninsula insulated the congregants from the buzz of the steadily building Saigon traffic beyond. Well-dressed families with children smiled, talked, and seemed happily ignorant of their current world, having spent the last hour contemplating the next one. I saw Thomas on a bench at the edge of the park. He was smiling broadly and seemed to be bantering with a group of children while their parents visited. He was completely engaged with the kids and hadn't seen me.

Thomas looked great. He was not in uniform; he wore a typical Vietnamese open-collared shirt hanging loosely from his square shoulders. He was lean but seemed more highly muscled than I remembered him. His joyful eyes darted between each of the children as he entertained them. I watched them until the families reformed. Thomas sat there alone for a moment as if savoring the scene before it left him forever. Then he looked up at me and shot off the bench toward me. He reached me before I could take two steps in his direction.

"Welcome to Vietnam!" he said, offering me his hand.

"Thanks. It's just a tropical paradise, isn't it?" I said, trying for sarcasm.

"It is," he said sincerely. "It's the most amazing country on earth. I love it here."

We hesitated, and then he walked back to the bench. I followed him.

"It's been a while, hasn't it?" I opened the conversation again. I was feeling a distance that I didn't enjoy with him.

"Over three years now."

"You don't look any worse." I laughed.

"You don't look any better." He laughed too.

He made no mention of why he left three years ago.

Sitting, I saw a wide scar on the interior of his forearm that went from his wrist to nearly his elbow.

"That's new since I saw you," I said, pointing to the scar. "Did you get a medal for that one?"

Thomas looked at me with a quiet calm in his eyes.

"No," he paused. "That was a civilian action from a while back."

"Let me guess," I said. "You cut your arm doing sheet metal work."

"Yeah, that's right. But it's not worth going into that story now."

"Okay," I said after a pause. "Art sent me a letter last month."

"Good. How are all the boys?"

"They all seem to be doing just fine," I said. "Pete had pneumonia last winter and needed a few weeks in the hospital. Art says he's fully recovered now. Ben had to leave town for a few months to help look after his grandchildren. His son died of a heart attack, and his daughter-in-law needed help. Ernie and Art just keep going."

"How's the team going to do this year?" he asked.

"Sorry. I really haven't been following them."

"You know, you're a pathetic excuse for a graduate of that great institution. You're in the states and you can't follow the team. Don't tell me; let me guess. You have no time because you follow Ivy League football now." His voice lifted as he warmed up.

He remembered from our correspondence that I took a journalism masters at Columbia.

"Yeah, that's me—Lions and Tigers and Bears and a few other mascots that are harder to define."

There was a lull in our conversation while half a dozen trucks with troops drove past. We both watched, each reading different stories in the faces of the men on the benches.

"How are you doing ... you know, with the emotional stuff over here? Do you still get depressed?" I was embarrassed, but I had to ask.

"I'm over all that stuff," he said without hesitation. "It sounds ironic, I know, but you eat, drink, do your job, and stay alive. It doesn't leave me much time to worry about the other things."

I nodded but didn't understand him beyond the words.

"What is your job?"

"Well, I've done a lot of things here, but now I count trucks."

"What does that mean?"

"It means 'I count trucks.' It's pretty simple, Julian, even for an Ivy League journalist. I start with 'one' and I stop when they stop."

"Where do you count trucks?"

"I hang my hat in a beautiful spot up north. I'm in Quang Tri these days."

"That's Indian country, isn't it?"

"Let me tell you a little secret: all of Vietnam is Indian country. We're here to do a job, but we aren't going to be here forever. If the local good guys don't stand up to the bad guys—and they have some seriously bad people trying to take over—then nothing we do here makes any sense."

"Back home, they say it makes no sense now."

He smiled. "What do you expect ... journalists. I don't need to read it. I see it myself."

"When you're not counting trucks?"

Another pause.

"What unit are you with?"

"I started out in a recon company in the Third Marines. But they bounce me around now. I often work alone. My unit usually doesn't have much to do with me, except for special assignments. I walk in the woods and check out what's going on in the villages. I spend most of my time in the woods."

"It almost sounds peaceful."

"That's absolutely right. I'm Henry David Thoreau with an M-40 rifle. I'm really more of a transcendentalist and naturalist than a marine."

"How is your Vietnamese?"

"It's passable. I even have a few Vietnamese jokes in my repertoire."

15

"Did the marines send you to school?"

"Yes, but not in languages. I picked up most of that myself. You just have to get in the right rhythm to pick out the words."

"Like music?" I offered.

"Yes, like music," he said.

We both paused. I think we were both thinking of the same piano a long way from there.

Then I said, "Why aren't you an officer? You must have been asked."

"I was, right after basic. It seemed like too much of a commitment at the start. Remember, I'd have to finish my degree. Then I found that I enjoyed being on the team rather than leading the team. I also realized I was happy not doing paperwork."

The morning sun was starting to bake as it rose overhead.

"I'll tell you what else I do when the trucks aren't rolling," he started again. "You remember me telling you what my favorite movie was?"

I didn't. I shook my head.

"I didn't think so. You don't follow the team. And you don't remember the important stuff."

"Okay, what was your favorite movie?"

"Well, it's the same movie, twice—*The Seven Samurai* or *The Magnificent Seven*. Actually, that's what I do. When Charlie comes knocking and the folks don't want to buy, well, Charlie sometimes has methods that can be brutally persuasive. Charlie could write a whole volume in the encyclopedia of torture."

"And you charge in and stop him?"

"No, no, no, this is Vietnam. Asian subtlety is required. I wait patiently until Charlie is in a clearing, preferably on a clear day without wind, and stop him from doing it again. It usually slows up his subordinates as well."

I waited a few moments, taking it in.

"Do you like what you do?"

He did not hesitate. "No, but I'm good at it." Then he added, "It's a job. I'm one of those people doing the hard things so that good people can rest easy in the night."

"I imagine it breaks up the monotony of truck counting?"

"It does."

We sat a minute quietly watching the traffic.

"Since you were asking," he began, "I do have another job— actually moonlighting."

"What's that?"

"Well, contrary to what you might read in your newspapers, when our fliers get shot down even in the north, their parachutes don't always bring them down right on top of a NVA platoon. They usually land out of sight and someone has to pluck them out. The air force and navy don't have the assets on the ground to do this. They go to the CIA and, listen to this: the navy actually pays in gold to get these guys out. Anyway, depending on the landing area, the CIA needs to look for subcontractors. Sometimes they sub it out to me. They're pretty generous paying for the help."

"So you're living large in Quang Tri?"

"Yes, but not in the way you think. My moonlighting employer has a pretty good money-movement system, and Mom has been able to draw money out of an account from an international bank in Chicago. I'm able to take care of her and a few other responsibilities as well."

"So that's the job?"

"Yes, but I leave a little time to be active in the Khe Sanh gardening club, and occasionally I have lunch with the girls in the village at bridge club. If it's not the rainy season, we have sampan races at the yacht club on the river on Thursdays after work. Also, my Rotary Club is heavily involved in a major replastering and repainting project in Hue. Time passes pretty quickly."

17

"I'm delighted you're keeping busy."

Thomas smiled and nodded.

"You must be coming up on the end of your tour?" I said after a pause.

"Well, not really. I re-upped last month."

"Don't you want to come home?"

"For the time being, I'm married to the marines. Mom and Indiana will have to wait. I tell you, though, I almost cry every day missing Mom and the farm. But I have a job to do here, and I know for sure that if I'm not here, it doesn't get done."

"Thomas, we do have thousands of marines over here."

"Yes, but none of them will do what I do."

I didn't challenge that comment, and we sat quietly for a minute or two. We watched a large family walk in front of us in the square. Another Mass was starting, and the parishioners were dribbling in. He spoke some greeting to the children passing in front of our bench, and they smiled at him. "Are you going to see Mom again anytime soon?" he continued.

"I have to be in Chicago next month on business. I'm going to drive down and meet her for dinner."

"Thanks. It's a great comfort to me to know that you're looking in on her." He paused for effect. "You make sure you keep watching out for her."

I nodded. "I will," I said sincerely. "I speak with her about twice a week when I'm back in the states. She obviously misses you terribly, but she also understands that you feel you need to be here."

"I know. When I flew her to Hawaii a few months ago to meet me on extended R&R, we talked, and she knows I'm going to be here for a while longer."

Thomas went quiet for a time and then abruptly said, "Let's go for a walk. I have an errand to run." He picked up the large nylon sack he had with him.

We left the church park and began a brisk walk around the city. Although a little out of breath, we talked about how bizarre it seemed to be catching one another up on events in Indiana as we paced down the side alleys of Saigon. We walked for about twenty minutes, out of the center of town toward the river. I had no idea where I was and made him promise to get me back before he left. Eventually we came upon his destination.

We came to an industrial area dense with small single- and two-story factories. Nestled among them was an outwardly similar building but with a children's playground on the side. Dozens of kids were in the playground, and several others milled about on the small shaded porch at the building's entrance. Thomas entered first and was greeted warmly in Vietnamese by a frail old woman. She had two toddlers at her feet. One of the kids had huge burn scars on her face and legs. The other child was missing an arm. The woman led us into the building. I noticed that many of the children milling around, most of them under five, bore some scar, amputation, or disfigurement.

She took us to a ward with ten beds going up each side of the room. Most of the beds were empty, although I assumed that their evening occupants were outside playing. Reading my face, Thomas provided an explanation.

"About half of these kids were in a hospital for their treatment before coming here. They will be recuperating here and then hopefully either going home to parents or to some family who will take care of them. A good percentage of them are orphans or abandoned."

The old woman led us further into the ward. We were joined by two other women who seemed to know Thomas. We stopped first at the bed of a little girl. Thomas leaned over and spoke to her quietly in Vietnamese. She seemed to recognize him, and she was comfortable with him being so near. Both of her legs were bandaged. One was amputated below the knee. He reached into the sack and pulled out

19

a colorful paper mask. She was delighted. He said a few more words to her and then went on to the next occupied bed. This little girl had a bandaged face. He gave her a gift as well. We went into two wards. He gave all the children a paper mask, a silly animal hat, or a kite—if they might ever run again.

After seeing all the children, he had a final meeting with the old woman in her office. I stayed outside the door while he spoke with her. Although the door was partially closed, I saw Thomas hand her a large wad of bills and was able to read the gratitude on her face. She gave him a dignified hug and said good-bye. He came out with the empty nylon sack. He said nothing, and we walked to the street. A tear coursed down one cheek as he left.

We started walking again, and we said nothing for several blocks. I started to recognize where we were.

After walking a little further, I asked, "Do you want to come back to my hotel to grab lunch?"

Thomas hesitated and then said, "No, I don't do the Rex Hotel. That's officer and journalist territory. I start to itch when I go near there." He smiled. "Besides, I've have to go back up-country today. I have to go home." He checked his watch. "I leave in an hour to catch my plane."

"I'm sorry we couldn't visit longer."

"Yes, me too."

"I'm told that I'll be coming back in a few months," I said. "Maybe we can arrange a longer visit next time?"

"I look forward to it. You know where to write me."

I hugged him before he started to walk away.

"Take care of yourself," I said as the inanity of the cliché caught me. "Don't get hurt."

He paused and then said, "I may get killed, but I won't get hurt. They can only hurt you if you let them in." He paused. "They can kill you but they can't hurt you unless you let them in."

20

Thomas placed his hand on my shoulder, smiled, and walked off, but then he hesitated, turned, and asked me, "You said the Rex, right?"

"With the officers and journalists."

"Yes, I remember." He paused, thinking. "Look, book a table at seven o'clock tonight. I'll see what I can arrange."

Anna arrived a little after seven. I left my name at the podium, and she found me seated at a side table in the bar. She was beautiful, although her conversation was formulaic until the second round. She was Canadian and a nurse at a Catholic orphanage down toward the Delta. By that time, it was obvious we would not be seeing Thomas that evening. When she came in, I actually never thought that he would be joining us. She didn't seem surprised or otherwise disappointed that he wasn't coming. She was happy to have a nice bottle of wine and a good meal.

She started telling me about her time in Vietnam. Her war testimony was an unapologetic paean to our mutual friend. In addition to Thomas's battlefield exploits, he spent a lot of energy getting crippled and wounded children into care centers. She had worked up north at another hospital until a few months ago and had seen him frequently there. Either directly or by proxy, he managed to shuttle scores of kids in for treatment or placement. He helped children who otherwise would have been abandoned or whose medical conditions would have gone unattended.

Thomas had set this up well. He clearly wanted me to know about the kids, and the nurse was happy to tell the story. He is an amazing guy, she told me. No one else could have done it. I smiled and then recited a quotation that came to mind.

"He inclines to do something which is easy to him and good when it is done, but which no other man can do. He has no rival."

I smiled at her. "It's Emerson. Thomas and I have a mutual friend who loves Emerson, and he would have said that about Thomas if he were here listening to your story."

"It's not just a story. All that I told you is true."

"I have no doubt."

"He doesn't do any of this for any recognition. He just does it."

I nodded and then quietly added another line, "The less a man thinks or knows about his virtues, the better we like him."

"Is that Emerson, too?" she asked.

I nodded again.

"Maybe I should be writing Thomas's story instead of the drivel I write now."

"Maybe you should," she said earnestly.

I paused, thinking about what she said as she took another sip of wine.

"Let's go eat," I said. "He's not going to join us tonight."

We stood and she took my arm as we walked across the crowded bar. It was the beginning of something special. I wrote to her for almost a year before she came to the states. We dated a little longer and then were married. When I see it from a forty-year perspective, I suppose I was just another wounded child Thomas saved.

CHAPTER 3

I met Thomas during my last semester of college. After I missed an entire semester because of a serious automobile accident a year earlier, I looked to complete my credits that fall. I had suffered a head injury, and my recovery was slow. Although there were no outward signs, the accident left me nearly blind in one eye. It took some time to make the adjustment, but generally speaking, my vision gave me little difficulty as long as I wore my glasses. My biggest disappointment was that all my closest friends had graduated without me.

Because of the additional semester, there were more tuition bills to pay. I needed to find a job while I completed my degree. I returned in mid-August to look for work and housing. Near campus, there was an available unit in a house that had been converted into several small apartments many owners past. It had a bed, a hotplate, and a small sink and shower. There was no air conditioning, and the August heat in northern Indiana was brutal compared to the delightful summer I left in upstate New York. It was loud and dirty, but it was cheap and close enough to walk to campus, and I only had to rent it from August to December. It was going to be my last college home. Once I unpacked my car, I struck out for campus. The financial-aid office in those days doubled as a student employment agency, and I hoped some student jobs would be available.

I walked the tree-lined entry to the campus with the view dominated by its most well-recognized buildings. From a student perspective, the campus was still dormant. If one was not familiar with the population dynamics, the campus, with the university's focus on undergraduates, would seem nearly vacant. With students around the campus, it was beautiful; but without them, on a clear late summer's day, it was truly spectacular.

The campus was a large tranquil park. The lush, watered lawns were manicured without weeds or any hint of trash. There were two small sailboats on one of the two lakes beyond the carefully planned quadrangles. Flowers were blooming in their beds. There were few roads and fewer cars to break the peace. The only undergraduates in any numbers were the fall athletes, and by far the football team was the largest contingent. The setting combined with the population of the athletes made it seem like another race of people—mixed in color, but stronger and taller than the rest of us—lived in this idyllic place, secluded from the imperfect world.

I postponed my job quest to sit by the lake and take in the peace. An author said of this place that there was "blood in the bricks," and as I sat on the bench looking at the water and the buildings in the background, I felt it too. A few of my classmates had been drafted after graduation, and a few others were on ROTC scholarships. They were all in uniform now. It was strange how far away all the conflict of the war seemed from that bench. It was stranger still to feel how alive my memories of them became by coming back to this place. I felt otherwise less connected with the university than I had just three months ago. With that sad thought, I went to the student-aid office to look for work. On the way, I saw a few "End the War" signs posted around, but you almost had to look for them to notice.

I knew that would change when classes resumed, but I didn't miss either the signs or the students.

The financial-aid administrator was helpful. We talked about my course load and what type of jobs might work around it. We talked about my short-term financial need, which seemed to be greater than most students, and he asked me how much I wanted to make a week. When he heard the number, he smiled and reached into a file. He told me I could come close to that figure at the Hotel Lafayette downtown, which I had seen but had never entered. I called the hotel from his office. They could interview me later that afternoon.

The Lafayette was on one of the prime intersections downtown and reflected much of the personality of the town. The exterior was in many ways classy and classic. It was a solid brick mid-rise building with ornamental concrete lintels over the main entrances. The sweeping eyebrow Palladian window arches lined the whole street perimeter, and the wide sidewalks added to the illusion of grandeur—even with the flaking paint on the window frames. The Lafayette stood across the street from one of the town's main bridges. The hotel, like much of the town, had enjoyed its salad days decades ago.

As I approached the hotel's entrance, a workman about my age was adjusting one of the massive wood and glass front doors. The man was vaguely familiar, but I couldn't really place where I might have seen him before.

"Hi," I said to him. "I'm looking for Mr. Anderson."

"You must be the new night bellman," he said, smiling. He extended his hand to me. "I'm Thomas. I'm the hotel handyman. You'll find Hal waiting for you by the front desk."

"Thanks," I said and entered the hotel still trying to place where I had seen Thomas before.

The Lafayette's interior evoked a feeling similar to its façade. It must have been considered incredibly elegant decades earlier, but now it screamed its need to be redone. The central lobby ceilings were about twenty feet high. Their decorative friezes were still impressive as they framed the large rectangular entry, despite the graying plaster chips that hung like bark around them. In a corner was a grand staircase with a wide landing leading to the mezzanine. Opposite the stairway, in a quiet seating area, stood a beautiful black grand piano. The whole scene was grandmother's parlor writ large, and seeing it made me instantly both happy and sad.

The main desk anchored the view in the lobby. In front of the desk, the hallway to the coffee shop, bar, elevators, and gift shop fed off to one side and to the main dining room on the other. The only people in the lobby were two men, one in his seventies behind the desk and the other in his fifties in front of it. The younger of the two seemed to be waiting for me.

He may have been in his fifties, but he talked as a much older, world-weary man.

His eyes locked onto me as I walked across the lobby, but he lowered them as he spoke.

"Are you the college student?' he asked.

I introduced myself and smiled at him.

"Okay, Julius, my name is Hal Anderson," he said. "You got the application?"

I did, and I handed it to him.

He spent a moment reviewing it before looking at the wall to my right.

"You meant to say your name was 'Julian,' right?"

Being polite, I agreed with him. "Yes, that's what I meant to say."

"What did they tell you about the job?"

"Forty hours a week or more, minimum wage, two meals a day, and you put a premium on reliability."

He took another long look at the one-page application.

"Yeah, that about covers it, although right now, it's a minimum of forty-eight hours and you might get more hours if you want them. We don't want to hire too many people." He said this thoughtfully and went back to reading the single sheet.

"What are you studying?" he asked as he read the page for what must have been the fifth time.

"History," I said, expecting to have to defend my choice of majors to him.

"That's pretty good. I read a lot of history myself. I like to read about World War II and Korea." His voice brightened slightly, but his expression didn't change. "Do you know much about Korea?"

"I read a lot more about World War II," I said honestly.

"I know about Korea—firsthand. I was drafted in '52. Not enough guys wanted to come out of mothballs from World War II. Who the hell would? Anyway, I went over there. I was scared to death, and then when I got that under control a little bit, I nearly froze to death. I tell you, I couldn't wait to come back to Indiana."

I nodded with all the empathy I could muster.

"Where are you from?" he asked.

"My family comes from upstate New York."

"Why did you come all the way out here for college? I don't imagine it was for the climate."

"No, it wasn't for the climate."

He dropped his eyes and I thought he was going to respond, but he didn't. He stared hard at me again. Then he took another look at the application.

"It says here you'll graduate this December and you can only give me four months." He paused. "If our other guy didn't just run off, we wouldn't be interested. I'm kind of in a pinch now, and you buy me a little time to look for another permanent guy."

"That's good for me, I guess."

"Yeah, good for you, bad for me. I'll have to do this all over again in a few months. But I imagine you won't have much choice wanting to stay after you graduate. I guess you'll be learning all about rice paddies pretty soon after that."

I didn't want to tell him about my eye and that the army had already made it clear they were not interested in having me in their future employ.

"I guess so," I agreed.

He examined my shoes again.

"Well, that's a damned shame you'll be going to Vietnam. Anyway, we have a few months to worry about it, right?" He almost smiled. "Well, let's talk about the job." He looked at me, and I nodded.

"First," he said, "let me tell you about the Hotel Lafayette." He paused. "As a history major, do you know anything about Lafayette?"

"The Frenchman in the Continental Army?" I asked.

"No, I don't think so," he said uneasily, I think not wanting to hurt my feelings. "You're right, he's French, but this was the Revolutionary War Lafayette. It was the US Army." He said this softly so I knew he was trying to make me feel less bad about my education.

"Okay, now I'm following you," I said.

"Well, it's not really important. I don't think he ever came to Indiana, and I don't know why it's named after him anyway. But that's who it is."

He paused and made eye contact with me.

Looking to his right, he continued. "Well, here's the story of the place. As you can see, it's an old hotel—maybe 1910, 1920. It's old. It's a landmark, really. I know a lot of it still looks old, but we have a new owner who's really putting some money in the place. The mezzanine and meeting rooms here," he stopped to gesture above, "will all be redone and modernized. The first two guest floors, numbers three and four, have already been completely gutted, and they're as good as any Hilton or Holiday Inn anywhere. They're working on fixing the fifth floor now. That should be done in the spring. If it all goes well, we'll be completely repainting the lobby next summer. It's too bad you'll be gone, but ..." He paused for effect. "When you get back from the jungle, it'll all look pretty good to you. You can bet on that."

I continued to nod, showing that I was interested, still interviewing to get the job.

"So we have nine floors; ground, mezzanine—where my office is if you ever need me—and then seven guest floors. The first two guest floors are for high-paying guests, overnighters, except for the two girls who live there full-time—you'll learn more about them later. The next floor, number five, is being worked on. We'll get some overnighters on six and seven when two and three spill over. We save eight and nine for the long-term guests—the full-time residents. We only have two of them now. You'll get to meet them later. During the college functions like graduations, we fill all the floors up. We're trying to have number five done by graduation this year."

He looked up at me and then paused as if he was trying to remember if there was anything he'd missed.

"So that's the hotel. You have any questions?"

"No." I shook my head.

"Well, let's talk about the job then."

"Sure."

"First, Julian, if you don't mind me asking, why do you have to work?"

"Well, Mr. Anderson, I suppose—"

"Call me Hal."

"Hal, I'm in debt up to my eyeballs, and I'm not done with school yet."

29

"How much are you going to be able to work?"

"I can work full-time. That's why I'm here."

"That's good. Like I said before, we might even be able to give you overtime on weekends with better tips if you want it. The nice thing there is you don't have to commit to it. Just show up; there's always something to do on Saturdays."

"That sounds good to me, Hal."

"Good." He started to look a little nervous, and this time he looked to the ceiling.

"Have you ever had any trouble with the police?"

I hadn't.

"No drug problems?"

"No, I'm clean."

Hal seemed satisfied.

"Good, here's the job. We call you a night bellman, but really there's not too much 'bellman' about it. You do a little of everything, and mostly you're there to help Max—he's the night desk clerk—if he needs anything. Are you following this?"

I nodded.

"You carry anyone's bags if they need you to. It's pretty quiet around here most nights, so the work isn't that hard. You'll be the room service waiter up until about eleven when Mike shuts down the bar." He looked at me and paused. "You are twenty-one, aren't you?"

"I'm twenty-two."

He looked down at the application again. He seemed to be doing the arithmetic with my birthday in his head.

"Well, besides room service, the guests always seem to come up with some errands for you. Some make sense; some don't. If you have any questions, ask Max. We generally try to do a little more for the resident guests. Max can help you with this."

"All right."

"Mostly, you're here to keep Max company. You and Max are the only ones on duty from midnight, when the bar closes, until six when housekeeping starts to show up. By the way, have you been in any fights lately?"

"No. My last fight was when I was in fourth grade. I was punched out by a sixth-grade girl." I paused. "Why do you ask?"

"Sometimes, there's some, let's call it 'bouncer' work here, especially when it's cold and the street people want to flop in the lobby. It's really light bouncer work. Most of the time you just, you know, coax the drunks out of the lobby or off the sidewalk. If you need the cops, Max will call them. They're pretty quick."

I didn't say anything.

"Are you still interested?"

"I am. You didn't scare me off."

"Good. Here's your schedule. We need you here working from seven at night to seven in the morning Monday through Thursday, and depending on the weekend relief man, sometimes Friday night, too. You can work out any other switches with the weekend man if you can both agree—he's pretty easygoing. Also, if you want to have dinner here, come in a little early. The kitchen guys will try to leave something out for you between six and seven. You can have whatever they put out; although on Sunday, if you want to come in, you can show up in the dining room and order off the menu—I'd recommend doing that. If you want a snack after hours, I don't care. Just don't go crazy. It's only you and Max, and after fifteen years here, I know he don't eat much." Hal looked me in the eye when he paused.

Looking away, he started again.

"From seven to midnight, you'll do mostly room service jobs unless the bar or Max needs you to do something else. When it quiets down after midnight, you have to vacuum the lobby, empty the ashtrays, and do any other cleaning that's really necessary—like if someone tracks mud on the rug or worse."

Pause and eye contact, again.

I nodded.

"Like I said, any bums come in, you gotta toss them out, and I don't care how cold it is. Cops will help you if you need them. If anything goes wrong with the plumbing or electric or whatever that you can't make right, unless it's really an emergency, don't worry about it. Thomas is the handyman, and he comes in at eight the morning. He can deal with most anything that goes wrong. Are you still with me?"

"Yes, I'm still listening."

"Now the best part is after you finish the clean up, you're on the downhill run. You can sit, sleep, or read until five, five thirty. Then you walk down to the post office and bring up the mail. A one-block walk at five AM will help you wake up to start your day. About five thirty, the papers come, and you should bring them in off the street, undo the bundle, and split them up between the coffee shop, the front desk, and the gift shop."

Pause and then nod again.

"Now the bakery delivers at six. They bring bread and pastries for the coffee shop that opens at six thirty. By the way, it's okay to pinch a few donuts in the morning. We figured in extra since the night bellman will take them anyway. At seven, you can leave or you can stay and have breakfast in the coffee shop. I recommend the blueberry pancakes. Any questions yet?"

"No questions."

"Last thing is like I said. Unless you switch your schedule, you have Saturday and Sunday nights off unless you want to come in on Saturday. We always seem to have something to do on Saturday—day or night, and I'll pay you time and half and you have better tips too."

"That sounds great."

"Well, it's not really great, but you're gone in four months."

"Yes, I am."

"Now let me show you where to pick up your uniform."

Hal walked to a small room behind the front desk and opened the door to a narrow closet. He pulled out a red vest with gold buttons.

He walked back with it and made me put it on.

"You look good in that," he said almost proudly.

I didn't know how to take the compliment.

"Can you start tomorrow?" he continued.

"Yes, I'll be here tomorrow night at six."

"Good. I'll show you the kitchen now. Are you hungry, Julian?"

CHAPTER 4

I learned early at the Lafayette that my job had very manageable expectations and no pressure. The prevailing work ethic was to do the minimum job and nothing more. However, the duties were well compartmentalized, and there was always a person, however poorly motivated, ready to do their minimum. My classes had not yet started, and I enjoyed having something prescribed for me to do.

With this management standard, the Hotel Lafayette ran well—not quickly, not efficiently, but well. It was a case of under-promising and delivering to the letter. If a room service order was promised in forty minutes, it would never be ready in less than thirty-nine but never take longer than forty-five. If housekeeping was expected to clean and take out the trash on Mondays and Fridays, there was never a need to look for them on the other days. It was all like clockwork—a slow clock but always predictable. I quickly fell into the routine and organized my Lafayette life like the other employees.

The night barman was a housepainter when he wasn't serving drinks. The bar was a small room that really only sat ten people around the old cherry bar with its faded brass ornaments. It would open on time, never early or late, and would close immediately at the scheduled time—patrons or not. The manager of the coffee shop was a mother of three whose husband worked a swing shift at one of the local factories. She opened the coffee shop at 6:29 AM each day for the first 6:30 patron. She closed at 3:00 PM and never at 3:01. It was a little bit of Switzerland in northern Indiana, although the commitment to punctuality was more palpable than the commitment to quality.

Max also did bookkeeping and prepared tax returns when he wasn't working at the Lafayette. He had been at the Lafayette forever and seemed to be totally contented with his job. He wasn't much of a conversationalist, which I would come to appreciate through many a long, quiet night.

My first official duty on the job was to enjoy a free meal. Often, it was one of the specials from the dining room that didn't sell. Sometimes, when the special was especially popular, dinner was whatever the kitchen had left over. Not infrequently, it was a sausage link sandwich left over from breakfast chased by the precooked French fries they occasionally kept warm. I quickly tired of this meal and would take my revenge out on the dessert refrigerator. There was always an ample supply of pies, cakes, custards, and ice cream.

It was shortly after my first three-course dessert that I was summoned with my first call. Max took the call at the main desk. I was to take Mrs. Howard, one of our residents, a tray from the kitchen and a drink from the bar.

The requisite forty minutes passed before her tray was ready. I gathered her drink from the bar and was off. When I arrived, I found her door ajar.

"Come in," she said warmly and welcoming, lingering on both words. "You're the new boy Hal told us about. You're the college boy." She gestured me into her room, a one-bedroom apartment with a modest kitchenette with ancient appliances and peeling linoleum flooring.

She was dressed in a short, light bathrobe and small, pink slippers. The décor was a mix of hotel furniture and her knickknacks and photographs. She was old and frail but offered a quick smile.

"I'm sorry to be dressed like this, but it's too damned hot tonight to wear clothes." She gestured to her robe.

I stood there sweating. I agreed completely.

"Let's see what you have on the tray." She spoke to herself as she pulled back the linen cover draping the metal covers of each of the plates. "Yes, that's just what I wanted." She smiled at me again.

She turned, walked to the windowsill, and brought back a tray to me.

"Here's yesterday's dinner tray. I left your tip on the tray."

She held the door open for me as I left. She had placed a quarter on the tray for me. I smiled as well.

Max later explained that Mrs. Howard almost never left the hotel except to have her hair done. Other than this weekly trip down the block, she stayed in the hotel. She entertained no visitors.

She did have one friend in the hotel, I learned. He was my second call of the night about an hour after Mrs. Howard. He was much less complicated. His name was Jeffrey Granger. He was a widower resident on the same floor as Mrs. Howard. According to Max, Granger was about fifteen years younger than Mrs. Howard, but he looked to be in roughly the same state of repair. Max told me that they had installed additional smoke detectors on the floor after Granger moved in. He was a chain-smoking alcoholic who was estranged from his children. Max only knew this because they tried to move him out of the hotel a year ago. There was an intervention of sorts to make Jeff renounce his bourbon, cigarettes, and solitude. Two of Granger's children and four of his grandchildren came to make the extraction, but he resisted. Jeff eventually called the police, and the family received the message. He had a difficult time after that, but he and Mrs. Howard became friends; they would visit in the lobby on Wednesdays.

Granger didn't smoke in Mrs. Howard's company. She made no secret of her feelings about the smoke, and for at least an hour or so on Wednesday afternoons, he respected her wishes. His love for tobacco and her strong feelings to the contrary made any gossip about additional trysts between them too ludicrous to consider.

I was to bring Granger a bottle of bourbon. The service bar did not stock his brand, and I had to walk to the liquor store just down the block to buy it. Granger, as a full-time resident, merited this service.

When I came to his room, he answered the knock promptly. "My name is Jeff," he said, extending his boney hand with a yellow index finger. "Do you want to come in a have a drink?" He hungrily took the bottle I had just brought. The television was loud in the background, and I had to shout to be heard.

"No thanks; another time."

"You come up after work sometime."

"I get off work at seven in the morning."

"Don't matter," he said. "This bar has no last call, and it opens early." He smiled a full denture smile as I retreated.

"Thanks. Maybe I will. I'll see you later, Jeff."

"See you later, kid. Thanks for the booze." He abruptly turned and shut the door in my face.

I left without a tip. Max told me later that Granger never tipped. His bourbon was tacked on to his monthly bill. I could expect about five runs a week for Jeff. Two or three would be for alcohol, the remainder for cigarettes.

There were no more calls the rest of the first night. I raided the kitchen for a snack about midnight, and Max and I finished the last piece of apple pie they had in the refrigerator. After the snack, I pulled out a book, located a comfortable chair, and relaxed in the quiet lobby. Max had to complete the day's invoices and prepare the morning billings. There were only about a dozen guests in the hotel beside the residents. The hotel would fill in the next week when the college freshmen's parents arrived, but until then it would be restful.

I started my deep-night routine at about three. I was bored with my book and actually didn't mind the lobby clean-up job. Trash removal, ashtray cleaning, and the minor dusting went quickly. I rolled out the vacuum and had completed the hallway carpets when two women and a man I hadn't seen before walked into the lobby.

The man and one of the women looked to be about thirty-five. The older woman was a buxom peroxide blonde. The other woman was younger, lean, and looked almost prepubertal. They stopped and hovered around me as I worked. I turned off the vacuum since they seemed to want to talk.

The man smiled at me. "I'm Marco," he said. "I live on three."

"Nice to meet you."

"This is Sherlene," he said, pointing to the older women. "And this is Eileen."

"Nice to meet you all," I said with as much enthusiasm as the hour would allow.

The women smiled but said nothing. They looked tired.

"We all live on three. Hal told us about you starting," continued Marco. "How's the first day on the job?"

"It's all right. No surprises. Just like it was described."

"Good," said Marco. "We're going to bed now. We won't have any surprises for you tonight either. Nice meeting you." Marco waved to Max, who waved back.

With that they summoned the elevator and disappeared into the cab.

I finished my vacuuming and walked back by the lobby desk. I think Max saw my expression when I spoke with the three.

"They're residents," he said. "They're also hookers, but that's not our problem. They don't work here; they just live here."

"How long have they been living here?" I asked.

"The guy, Marco, and Sherlene have been coming around here for a few years now. They come here at the start of the summer and leave about Thanksgiving. I don't know where they go after that. The young girl is new this year. I don't know how she fits in." He paused. "I heard them say that they work out of a hotel out west down by the airport."

"What does Hal say about it?" I asked, probably a little naïvely.

Max smiled and said, "He doesn't care what they do or who they are as long as they pay their bills and they don't do anything illegal here."

I didn't respond right away.

"Don't they offend the other guests?" I eventually asked.

"From what I can see," said Max, "they're either in their rooms or out of the hotel. The only time they usually end up in the lobby is coming or going, and half of that is in the middle of the night. Also, let's face it, kid—we don't have a lot of other guests most of the time." He paused again. "Do you have a problem with any of that?"

"No, I guess not." I walked away with my vacuum feeling a little more worldly.

The rest of the night passed as per Hal's script. The mail was collected, the newspapers gathered and distributed, and the donuts found, and I levied the small carrying charge that was expected. I had breakfast in the coffee shop and had finished my first day. It was all new but somehow already comfortably familiar.

After breakfast, I said good-bye to Max for the day and was walking out when I saw Thomas arrive. He was dressed in his khaki uniform with a tool belt on his waist.

"How is it going so far?" he asked.

"After one night, I'm still here."

"Are you still a student, working all these hours?"

I was feeling very tired at that moment and loved the sympathy.

"Yes," I said wearily. I had not yet established my sleep schedule, and I was exhausted.

"Well, this place will broaden your education. There's no doubt about that. Say, do you want to grab some coffee before you go?"

"Thanks," I said. "But I'm really asleep on my feet. Let's do it another time."

"Sure, I understand," he said and then walked away.

I knew I had seen him before, but I couldn't place where.

CHAPTER 5

The rest of the week passed quickly. It was largely the same routine, right down to the calls from Mrs. Howard and Jeff Granger. I bumped into Marco and the girls a few more times as well. I think I gained a few pounds; what I was missing in drinking beer with my classmates, I more than balanced with free sausage sandwiches, desserts, and morning donuts. It was Saturday on Labor Day weekend. Freshman orientation had come and passed, but there were still a few parents staying at the hotel on the refurbished floors.

Classes began the next week, and I really didn't have much going on. While I was not the rabid football fan I had been as a freshman, I did pay sufficiently close attention to know that the first game was not until the following week. Given that I had time on my hands, I told Hal that I would work the day shift on Saturday. He was relieved because the usual day man was not coming in.

The day routine was a little less structured than my nightshift. Essentially, the day bellman was at the beck and call of the guests and management with little scheduled. Even the meal breaks were largely catch-as-catch-can, which was a small jolt to my now-established foraging habits.

Joe was Max's day relief man. During the busiest time, from late morning until mid-afternoon, Hal came over to work with Joe. I was thrown off by the lack of routine. I now expected my call from Mrs. Howard, whom I started to think of as a cute old lady. I could take or leave Granger, but I didn't hear anything from him either.

The morning passed quickly, with multiple checkouts and several room service breakfasts in the lower two guest floors. Lunch was also busy, as there was a touring Broadway show in town at the Municipal Theatre down the block. The traveling players were staying at the Lafayette and all wanted lunch at about the same time so they would be ready for the matinee performance. The room service activity started to taper off about one, and it was peaceful by two.

Just as I caught my breath, Joe took a call. One of the residents on three had a request, and since it was slow again, I was to take care of it. It wouldn't be busy again until after the matinee performance, and I had a few hours.

On the third floor, I knocked on the door. The young woman I usually saw just before dawn greeted me.

"Hi," she said. "Come in."

I walked into her room, which was really just a hotel room unlike the apartments on the upper floors.

"Hi," she said again. "I'm Eileen. I usually ask the other guy this, but he's not here." She smiled as she flicked her hair over her shoulder. "Do you have time to do a little errand for me?"

Joe had told me that I would have the time.

"Yes, sure," I said.

"Well, can you go across the street to the Algonquin and get me a pulled-pork sandwich?"

"That's easy enough," I said.

"Thanks," she said. "I also need you to buy me fifteen rubbers in their vending machine."

"Fifteen rubbers?" I repeated.

"Yes," she said and smiled innocently, "and a pulled-pork sandwich, okay?"

"Okay," I said. She handed me some bills and off I went, unsure how I felt being an accessory to all of this.

When I walked by the lobby desk, I passed Joe. He was smiling. "Do you know where the Algonquin is?" he asked.

I did.

The Algonquin was directly across the street from the Lafayette. I had never been there before that day. The place was nondescript from the outside. It displayed less neon than many of the restaurants in the area. Inside, there was a small crowd. The lighting was subdued but not dark. The bar was U-shaped surrounded by tables lining both sides. The open end exited to the kitchen. A modest single television was mounted from the ceiling near the closed end. The clientele was generally young, working class, and male, although a few older men were scattered around. In one of the far corners, near the restrooms, sat four old men playing cards.

I noticed Thomas, in regular clothes, talking with a woman about my age in a waitress uniform. He was on the other side of the room from the card players. I was on my way over to say hello when I noticed the old men suddenly paying close attention to me.

The three old men facing me locked their eyes on my every step. The fourth turned after a moment or two with just as intense a gaze. I walked to the bartender and asked for the sandwich. He nodded as if he were expecting the order. I asked the barman to change the bill Eileen gave me, and again it seemed he was expecting this. I looked up and no longer saw Thomas, so I resumed my assigned task. I saw where the restroom was and started toward it, passing by the old men to get there. The chubby little man closest to me smiled.

"Grace and peace be with you, young man," he said, still smiling.

"Uh, thanks." I wanted to be done with this errand, and I kept walking.

"Please sit down a moment with us," said one of the others.

"Well, I can't, really. I'm working."

"It's all right," said the third. "The sandwich won't be ready for a few minutes."

"Well, I have to do something while they're fixing the sandwich."

Then the last man spoke to me. He was by far the most physically intimidating of the old men.

"Don't worry, son. You sit. Joe won't miss you."

Whether because of his mention of Joe or the commanding tone of his voice, I obeyed and pulled up a chair. I now noticed Thomas walking out the door as I pulled in my chair. He waved to the table with a smile as he walked to the door.

The four men all smiled at me as I settled into the chair. The command voice belonged to the largest one, who had a completely bald head. Two were lean, and the other was unpleasantly fat. One of the two thin ones had a full beard that had grown to touch his chest.

"I work across the street," I said lamely, remembering too late that I was wearing the hotel's red vest.

"We know that," said the command voice.

"We know your name is Julian," said the short fat one.

"We also know that you are currently the young factotum for Lemon Top," said the bearded one.

"Lemon Top?"

"The young lady in the hotel," he added.

"Oh, yes … I am."

"And you are on an errand to fetch appliances for the boomslangs of milady's gentlemen. Correct?"

After thinking about this phrase for a moment, I said, "Yes. How do you know this?"

"Oh, we know many things; too many, I'm afraid," said the bearded one. "The panjandrums who run the student affairs office are also known to us, us to them, and now you to us as well."

"You signed a release with your application," said the large man by way of explanation.

I didn't say anything for a moment as I thought about his the explanation.

"We seem to have you at something of a disadvantage, young man," said the clean-shaven thin man. "Allow me to make our introductions around the table." After pausing to see that I was paying attention to him, he continued.

"This stout man to my immediate left," he said as he gestured, "is Peter. To Peter's left with his druidic facial hair is our late-in-life bohemian, Ben. Art is our clean-shaven partner. I am Ernie. We are all former schoolteachers, although Art sadly left the academy many years before his prime to undertake more philistine endeavors."

Ernie turned to Art and said, "We are now enjoying the fruits of those wanderings."

I must have looked puzzled.

"I own the place," explained Art. I now remembered that I had seen Art in the hotel talking with Hal earlier in the week.

"Can we offer you something to drink?" asked Peter.

"Well, I should be getting back."

"Danielle." Art called to the young waitress who had been speaking with Thomas, ignoring my excuse, and I knew that any further demurrals would be futile.

It was worth it to see Danielle more closely. As she came up to Al, she flashed a perfect smile at the table. She was tall, healthy, and physically perfect by any criterion.

"Danielle." Al pointed toward me. "He needs a drink." All eyes turned to me. I ordered a soft drink and watched her walk away.

After she left, Ben, the man with the beard, was the first to speak.

"You must forgive us. We are a cabal of bored old men and love nothing more than to irritate young people. You are especially vulnerable to the klieg lights because of the rather debasing mission that you are on—and I don't mean the sandwich."

"That's true," said the pudgy man, Peter. "We, as the presbyters of this fine establishment, try to imbue the appropriate sense of probity for all activities coming and going. However, were it not for the refulgence of the lovely Danielle, the place would be a total loss, I'm afraid."

Art frowned and shook his head but said nothing.

Ernie seemed to sense that they were losing me and brought the subject around to one that I could better understand.

"How are you enjoying your work as a bellman?" he asked.

"Well," I said, "I won't make a career out of it, but it's a pretty good job for me now."

There was a pause as Danielle brought my drink and I thanked her.

"We understand that you come from New York State?"

"Yes," I said haltingly, still surprised at how much they knew about me.

"And that you have a midyear graduation."

'Yes, I had a bad car accident last year and had to miss the fall semester."

"And you don't think you will pursue the life of a bellman after you get your degree?" asked Ben.

I just smiled at him.

"Will our elected leaders' diktat not immediately reward you with a government job right after graduation?"

"No. I don't think the army wants me after my accident."

"That's a shame," said Peter. "You'll have to find another job." He gestured to my vest. "Well, at least you'll come out of college with a skill, which is more than most of your classmates can boast."

"I think I'm going to try to get in to a journalism masters program when I'm done."

"Staying within the bosom of the academy; highly laudable," said Ernie.

Danielle came over to me with the sandwich in a bag.

"Well, I'd better get back," I said as she brought the bag.

Ben commented next. "Lemon Top will keep; I wouldn't worry about her. Actually, if it were Melon Top, she likely would have forgotten already from what I've seen of their little fesnyng."

"'Melon Top' is the other girl at the hotel?" I asked, wanting to be sure.

"Yes," Ernie said. "You see, since we don't really get to meet these people and we only see them from afar, as it were, it is easier for us to identify them by their … uh … their entablatures." Ernie looked at the table, pleased at his word choice.

"Is that the right word?" he asked, almost looking for congratulations.

The other old men seemed to agree that it was.

I thought I understood him, nodding as I got to my feet.

"Ah, you have to go now," said Peter. "But as you go, I tell you that I think it's a low thing that you do—and I don't mean the sandwich either. The preacher tells us, 'Have no fellowship with the unfruitful works of darkness.' Perhaps it is a worthy saying both for bellmen … and for lonely young women."

Ernie spoke next. "You are a harsh judge, my friend. I fear she has unfortunately been groomed for this role by the hand of fate. The philosopher would tell us that 'the height of the pinnacle is determined by the breadth of the base.' I suspect that she was not molded with a firm base. Let us not judge."

"I do not judge, but I do observe, and it is makes me rather sad to see youth spent in such a way," responded Peter.

"It is sad, indeed," Ben concurred, "but *nil desperandum*. She is young, and for many, this is a world of second chances."

I was trying to get out of there before they continued this any longer.

As I backed from the table, Art spoke up in an even stronger version of the commanding voice he had used with me earlier.

I froze when I heard his voice, but it was not directed at me.

"Hey, Eddie," he bellowed. A huge man, perhaps a few years older than me, on the other side of the bar looked up. He had a large hunting knife with about an eight-inch blade in his hand. He had flipped it in the air and caught it before it hit the bar. He seemed to be showing a trick to the man he was drinking with.

"Eddie, put that damned knife away and don't take it out again. If you even think about playing mumblety-peg on my bar, you'll never come back in here, do you understand?"

Still frozen, I watched Eddie obediently put his knife back in the leather scabbard on his belt.

"He really is a dummy," whispered Ben.

"And a mean drunk," added Peter.

"Why do you tolerate him in here, Art?" asked Ernie.

Art looked at the three of them with a steady gaze.

"I think you know the answer to that," he replied and then continued after a pause, "I'm a forgiving man, and he's a good customer.

I started walking to the men's room to complete the other half of my mission.

"Hey, Julian." Art's voice stopped me in my tracks again. "Ask the bartender for a bag before you go to the vending machine. We don't want those things dropping all over the sidewalk when you leave."

CHAPTER 6

Classes started, but I was having difficulty returning to an undergraduate mentality. It was college, advertised as the best years of my life, but my mood was heavy with guilt for my friends who were now enlisted. For those of us left comfortably behind, there was a strong feeling that the world needed changing and most specifically that the United States needed to leave Vietnam. On all college campuses across the country, the incessant din of defeatism eventually tarnished any remaining quaint murmurs of patriotism.

I came to work on a Sunday night substituting for the weekend night bellman. The hotel was quiet. It was raining hard and it was warm, but there was a sense that now, in early September, harvest time was approaching in the Corn Belt. I was bored in the empty lobby and walked into the bar that, except for one patron, was just as quiet. The television was tuned to a news program. TV news somehow made it so that the newsmen were heroes and the soldiers were, at best, just extras in the act. I asked the barman to change the channel and found that the networks all had the news—and it was all the same story. Newsmen, trying to look brave standing in rice paddies, were intensely serious. Somehow I think it should have been pointed out that they were there because they wanted to be, not because they had been drafted.

I made my usual trips to Mrs. Howard's room for her supper and delivered cigarettes to Granger. The girls were in early that night, whether out of respect for the day or for the weather, I wasn't sure. Marco, Sherlene, and Eileen were rather subdued when they came in just before nine. The three shuffled by me in the hall without comment, although Eileen gave me a quick little smile as she passed.

I had some reading to do, so I finished my clean-up chores early and tried to attend to my studies. I found a comfortable chair and pulled out a book. I must have had too much fun earlier in the day, because I couldn't stay awake. I remember seeing twelve thirty on my watch, and then I don't remember. I lapsed into a deep sleep.

I awoke slowly, as if still in a dream. As I stirred, I was watching a concert. The sensation was pleasant. The music was lovely. It was piano music that called and cried and spoke to me in my dream. My shirt was sweaty and my body stiff from a short but deep sleep. The music continued.

I awoke further and looked at my watch. It was a little after three. I was surprised when I heard that the music was coming from the lobby piano. I could not see who was playing from my seat because the soundboard lid was in the way. I could see Joe at the lobby desk. The clerk was unconcerned by the player and he also seemed to be listening to the music as he completed his billings. I was torn as my curiosity to see the player fought my desire to reclose my eyes and simply savor the music and the moment. Inertia won, as it usually will at that hour, and I just listened and enjoyed.

When I checked the time again, it was nearly four. The player continued, and each new piece was more exquisite than the last. I knew a little classical music at the time. I had heard pieces by Chopin and Mozart. I had also heard a Tchaikovsky symphonic theme put to the piano. The clerk had disappeared from sight, and I felt that it was time to walk over and satisfy my curiosity.

I was stunned to see that the musician was Thomas, the hotel handyman. He was playing in part with his eyes closed or concentrating on the keyboard, but he did look up as I peered around the piano. He nodded to me, and I nodded back to him. He focused totally on the music and after the brief notice didn't look at me again. He kept playing, all from memory, and I sat in one of the wing chairs where I had a better view of him. His selection went from dulcet to dramatic. He played for another twenty minutes or so. In his last selection, he switched abruptly to a lovely, peaceful, and sorrowful work that I had never heard. He gently finished the piece and, still not looking at me, carefully pulled over the keyboard cover.

He stared at me for a few moments before he spoke. I was never one who was comfortable with any social transition, and I waited for him.

"I couldn't sleep," he said apologetically. "I hope I didn't wreck your night. Joe told me to play when I walked in. He said you needed to get up anyway."

"He's right," I said. "I need to start moving. Your playing was incredible. I really enjoyed it."

"Thanks," he said. "You know, you're the first university student Hal's ever hired. He made a point of it to tell me how enlightened he's become."

"I suppose it's a big responsibility being the first." I laughed. "Where did you learn to play piano like that?"

"That's a long story that I should tell you another time," he said, looking at his watch.

"Okay. Let's get together for that coffee you mentioned last week."

"Sure," he said, putting out his hand. "We should grab a coffee or maybe lunch some time."

"I'd like that. I'd like to learn what you were playing."

"In a few hours I may not be able to tell you exactly what the pieces were, but we can cover the highlights."

"The highlights will do just fine."

"Listen, I have to go. I'm supposed to be back here in a few hours, and I need to do some things at home before I come in. I'll see you later."

With that, he briskly walked out.

It was at that moment that I remembered where I had seen him before. I had never met him but I knew his face. A lot of people who followed college football around the country knew his face. It was during my sophomore year that it happened. He was a year ahead of me in school. He was the leading receiver on the football team and he was talked about as an All-American. Then, in mid-season, he left the team. He just dropped out of sight. The university said it was due to "personal reasons," which is what they usually said for anything that didn't involve an arrest or an overt disciplinary dismissal. Obviously, there was much speculation as to what actually happened. Everyone had a different story, from a date-rape incident to the birth of an illegitimate child to theft to cheating on a midterm. There must have been ten different versions of a rumor that each teller swore was true. No one really knew, and the university was mum. The football faithful were hopefully expectant for his return during the season, and then for the spring practice, and then for the following fall. It never happened. Then, like any hero, although sports heroes were more durable than most in those days, he faded and vanished.

I went over to the clerk behind the lobby desk.

"What do you know about Thomas?" I asked him as he was sorting the guest folios and invoices.

"Not much," he said. "He's pretty good at plumbing and electric. He's an average carpenter, and he isn't much of a sheet metal guy."

"Wasn't he a football player at the university?"

"I heard that. But I don't follow that stuff."

"Why did he quit football?"

"I never asked him."

"Did he get in some trouble with the police?"

"Don't know. Don't think so or Hal wouldn't have hired him."

"You ever spend much time talking with him."

"No. He's a day man. I'm a night man. I don't see him except from time to time when he comes in to play the piano when he says he can't sleep. I'll tell you, though, when he comes in to play, it's so pretty it makes me want to sleep."

"He does play beautifully."

"Sometimes he comes in with that girl who works across the street. She's pretty easy on the eye, that one. You know who I mean?" He paused. "Usually, though, when he comes in at night, he comes alone. He hasn't brought the girl around in a month or so." Then he shrugged his shoulders as a substitute for any real information.

"Oh, one other thing you should know. If you like his playing, come around on Wednesdays before supper. He plays for Mrs. Howard then. It's about the only time you'll see her out of her room. Now I have to get back to work." He turned back to his papers.

I took his cue. I went behind the desk, pulled out an umbrella, and walked out to pick up the mail, the papers, and the donuts. I looked forward to seeing Thomas again.

CHAPTER 7

I was finishing my breakfast in the coffee shop a few hours later when I saw him come in. He looked fresh, and his energy was a humbling counterpoint to mine. I waved to him, and he sat with me.

"Good morning," he beamed in a voice that seemed wrong for the hour. I began to wonder if I had hallucinated his presence the past night. He shouldn't have been so chipper.

"Good morning, yourself," I mumbled into my third cup of coffee.

"Do you always look so miserable at the end of your shift?" he asked. He seemed to want information rather than banter.

"I was kept up past my curfew last night. I went to this great concert. It was a total surprise."

"Yes, life does that to you," he said sympathetically. Then he added, "If you don't mind me saying so, if I looked so terrible after a shift, I might consider getting into a different line of work."

"Thanks for the advice. Would you like some coffee?"

"No, I'm just fine," he responded in a voice that left no doubt.

"I didn't remember where I had seen you before last night until you left. You went to the university, didn't you?"

"Yes, I spent a few years there before I decided it wasn't for me."

"You played football too, right?"

"Yes, I did. I'm over that too."

"You gave it all up."

"I did."

"What made you quit?"

He hesitated and then looked me in the eye. "My heart wasn't in it anymore."

"Why? You were a star."

"I didn't want stardom. I think I wanted something else."

"Everyone wants stardom."

"No, not everyone."

"What did you want to trade for it?"

"Peace, maybe. No pressure for a change."

"But you were the best when the pressure was on."

He shrugged his shoulders and didn't speak for a few moments. Then he changed tack. "What do you want in life? What would you sacrifice for it?"

I hesitated, giving it some serious thought. I had been wrestling with this question myself for some months.

"I think I just want to get my degree and go home for a while."

"That's a good, short answer, although it's not exactly a strategy. Where's home?"

"I live in upstate New York, near Binghamton."

"Oh, apple-knocker country," he said with the animation back in his voice. "Good for you. That's great. My family lives on a farm, and we have an apple orchard ourselves. You don't live on a farm, by any chance?"

"No, but my best friend from high school did. It was a beautiful at his place. He didn't have any apples though. His family had cows."

"We never had any cows," he said firmly. "We had some pigs for a time, but no cows."

"Where is home for you?" I asked.

"I'm almost a local. I don't have to go far to get back to my farm. I grew up about fifty miles from here."

"Do you go home much?"

"Yes, I do get back pretty often. My mother lives there alone, and I'm the only child. It's hard to ignore Mom."

"I understand. My mother died a few years ago, and if she were still alive, I would hope that I wouldn't ignore her."

"I'm sure you wouldn't." He glanced at the large clock in the coffee shop. "Hey, I have a leaky faucet to deal with. Try to get some sleep. You give the night shift a bad name."

With that he patted me on the shoulder and left.

I didn't see him again until Wednesday of that week. I arrived at the hotel early, in part to clear up an issue with my paycheck, but my greater reason was to listen to Thomas play the piano again. Hal said it would be worth the effort to come in early.

Never having been there before at this time on a Wednesday, I did not realize what I was missing. Apparently, the mini-concert would start at four thirty. Hal relieved Thomas early from his maintenance duties so he could perform for the guests. Actually, he let Thomas go early from his work so that Mrs. Howard could listen and not disrupt her evening routine, which centered around the local and national evening news on television followed by her dinner. She had made her needs known to Hal early in the concert series some months back.

After I straightened out my issues with the payroll lady I came to the lobby to watch the concert. I sat in the corner. At four twenty, Mrs. Howard came out of the elevator. She was dressed in her Sunday finest. The day bellman had arranged some chairs around the piano, and she proceeded directly to a chair next to the keyboard. Granger rode down in the same lift, although he peeled off into the bar and joined her just before the concert with a drink in his hand.

In addition to Mrs. Howard and Granger, several of the housekeeping staff loitered in the lobby for the event. Other clerical staff made their way down from the mezzanine. A few people came in from the street and sat in the remaining chairs. Several more standees appeared. Some of them were guests; some were street walk-ins.

Maestro Thomas appeared punctually and worked the crowd a little. He spoke to several of the housekeeping group and some of the kitchen staff. Then he stooped to give Mrs. Howard a quick kiss on the cheek. Even with her overly made-up face, it was obvious that she was blushing. Thomas was carrying a rather thick folder of sheet music this time. He next consulted Mrs. Howard for any requests and arranged the sheet music on the stand to accommodate her wishes. Then he began to play.

And oh, how he played. His selection covered classical, show tunes, movie themes, and popular music. He played with such emotion and energy that the room was tomb quiet even during the heavy classical pieces. More people came in from the street as the concert progressed, and no one left the room. Marco and the girls came in and hovered on the lobby perimeter. Even they stayed for the full show.

Thomas played for about forty-five minutes (Mrs. Howard liked to watch the first news at five thirty) and left to a spirited applause, again working the room as he departed. The crowd thinned immediately, although the bar business was a modest beneficiary of Thomas's draw. I walked across the street to the Algonquin since I had a little time before I would come back to the kitchen and eat before my shift.

I expected to see Thomas and Danielle at the Algonquin, but neither of them was there. The Algonquin benefited from Thomas's concert more than the hotel bar did. I saw many of the same walk-ins gathering there. Art was in a booth in the corner by himself reading with a coffee cup in front of him. He looked up as I came in and waved me over.

"How was the concert?" he asked with a smile.

"It was incredible. I think someday the hotel will need to have the police provide crowd control."

"Yes, he packs them in. He's a man of many talents," he said quietly.

I agreed.

"How are you getting along over there?"

"I'm doing fine. It's a great job for me. My class load is manageable, and I have time to read and even grab a little sleep most nights. I have no complaints."

He nodded.

"Where's the rest of the gang?" I asked him.

"Oh, they stay pretty busy. Since young Mozart started his Wednesday shows, the boys have shifted our weekday dinner night to Tuesday. They don't like the crowds in here. I'm sure they're out working now."

"I thought they were retired."

"Well, there's retired and there's retired. They're all 'emeritus,' which is academic speak for double and triple dipping from pension to visiting professorships to guest lectures. These guys are actually very much in demand. I don't know if you know who they are, but together they probably wrote something like thirty books. They've all held endowed chairs."

"What did they teach?"

"Let me start at the beginning. We were all assistant professors at the same time. We'd get together to play cards, usually bridge with our wives, although not all of us had wives. Ernie lost his wife to cancer when he was in his twenties and never remarried. Peter is a priest. Ben and I would bring our wives, and those two brought two more players. It's amazing for me to think we've been doing this for going on fifty years." He took a sip of his coffee.

"Ben lost his wife about two years ago. He was a professor of English and a world authority on American poetry. Ernie taught philosophy. Peter, whom I've actually known since I was an undergraduate, still works full-time in one of the parishes with the homeless. He was a professor of theology and spent a few years at the Vatican."

"What about you?" I asked.

"I was the practical one. I taught accounting. I left academia just after I was asked to fill out my forms for tenure. It was nice to be asked, but I didn't really want to make that trip any longer. So I went out and made money. I was lucky at real estate. I understood cash flow and depreciation. I started with apartments and then branched into shopping mall developments. I did pretty well."

"You own this restaurant, right?"

"Yes. The boys liked it, and I wanted to keep it the way they liked it. I didn't want it to turn into a biker bar or a disco or anything different."

"So you bought it for them?"

"No, I bought it for me, so I could entertain them on Wednesday nights—excuse me, now Tuesday nights—and Saturday afternoons."

I nodded.

"There's a lot you can do with money. Two things you can't do are to start over and to bring back what's gone. Most of us would swap every nickel for that chance. We all hope we're trading up in the next phase, but ..." He shrugged. I had nothing to add on that topic, and sensing the conversation to be over, I excused myself while Art went back to his newspaper.

The rest of the week passed quickly, and I stopped over at the Algonquin again on Saturday afternoon. The university was playing an away game that was broadcast on television. Art and the other men were playing cards in front of the television, and no one was allowed to sit near the bar in their line of sight. Danielle was on duty.

I sat at the bar close enough to hear the conversation of Art's table. They played euchre, which Ernie described as bridge for barflies. With each new hand, they would stand and change positions around the table. I didn't know what they were doing until I realized that they were taking turns at having their back to the television. They were all fans, and occasionally they would stop the game to watch an important play. Then they would rotate again. Peter claimed this was the most exercise he could tolerate, although he welcomed the workout.

Danielle, or "Dulcinea," as Ben addressed her, was obviously most attentive to their table. The day bellman walked in and ordered a pulled-pork sandwich to go when she was serving their table. Ernie mentioned the name "Lemon Top" while Danielle was there. Her expression changed immediately.

"What do you call me when I can't hear you?" she asked the table. It was playful and not defensive.

"Only the most lovely things," said Peter.

"Like what?"

"Splendid," said Peter.

"Spectacular," said Ernie.

"Magnificent," said Ben.

Art hesitated, and Danielle, tiring of this, interjected, "You can say whatever you want. You sign my check."

She walked by me, knowing that I was in earshot. "You keep your comments to yourself," she warned.

She looked across the room as Eddie came in. "Oh, there's trouble," she said almost to herself as she left the table.

From Eddie's demeanor and looks, it was obvious that the Algonquin was not his first stop that afternoon. He came in with another fellow who looked even worse. They sat at the bar drinking shots of whiskey with their beers. Eddie and his nameless friend spoke loudly, and they were only half-watching the football game. The old men were focused on the card game, even more so with the newcomer's arrival.

I finished the beer in front of me and said my good-byes to the table. Going to the exit, I walked next to Eddie's spot on the bar.

He turned to me as I walked past. To my surprise, he smiled.

"Hey, how's it going?"

"It's going fine. How's it going with you?" I responded.

"Good. Hey, where's the All-Star?"

"Who?" I asked.

"You know, piano boy from the hotel."

"I don't know. I haven't seen him today. Neither of us works on Saturdays usually."

"Oh." Then he turned to his friend, with the cheering from the television in the background. "Hey look—I told you they'd score."

He turned back to me. "Did you play any football?"

I told him I hadn't.

"I did," he said proudly. "I grew up around here and got a lot of scholarship offers. I was a tight end at Michigan State, but they moved me to tackle when I blew out my knee. Then I screwed it up again and couldn't play anymore." He turned back to the television for a moment and then back to me.

"You know, I would have kept playing. I didn't just quit like the piano boy." He turned back to the television and ordered another beer. He started talking to his friend, and I took my leave.

I had gone about ten steps out the door when I heard my name. It was Danielle. I stopped as she walked up to me.

"Julian, how is your job going?" she asked.

"It's a job. I have no complaints. I get to sleep while I'm getting paid, and I get free food. How's yours?"

"Mostly tolerable. Art's a good boss. I don't get free food, but I bet I make more money than you do."

"I bet you do. I'm sure you work harder."

"I wanted to ask you about Thomas," she said in an even tone, now getting to the meat of conversation.

"What can I tell you?"

"Has he seemed a little bit off to you?"

"I don't understand what you mean. You know, I really don't know him well at all."

"I thought you worked together."

"I work nights; he works days. We see one another as we come and go."

She thought about that for a moment.

"Well anyway," she continued, "he gets these spells where he can't sleep at night. He gets all wound up. I've never seen so much energy in one person when he gets going. That part's good, I guess. But then he talks but doesn't listen. Sometimes he gets in arguments with strangers for almost no reason."

"Well, I haven't seen that," I said. I was thinking that his motor was running a little fast the night he came in and played the piano, but I didn't tell her that.

"But, did he seem, you know, normal?"

"Yes and he gave the people a great little concert on Wednesday."

"I heard that. He's always good, you know."

She thought another moment or two. Then she thanked me and went back to the Algonquin.

CHAPTER 8

A few days later, Thomas burst in the coffee shop while I was enjoying my breakfast. I had not seen him since the concert. He wanted to get together for lunch, and we planned it for the next day. He arrived about fifteen minutes late, picking me up on a corner near my place. He drove me to a restaurant not too far from the campus. He seemed to want to show me where his apartment was. It was in an old Victorian house that had been converted into several units. He didn't stop the car for us to go in, but his place looked to be several notches above mine. He pointed it out to me from the street on the way to the restaurant.

When we sat down at a small table, he was calmer than he had been during the prior week. He spoke slower, anyway. He was warm, patient, and engaging. A few of the restaurant staff addressed him by name as he came in. I sensed that part of it was his former notoriety as a football star.

After we ordered our drinks, I asked, "Where did you learn to play the piano so well?"

He rocked his chair back on two legs and said, "My mom was a piano teacher. She was also the organist at our church. She made me learn to play even though my dad wasn't all that interested in seeing me behind a piano."

63

"What did your dad do?"

A look of pride came over Thomas. "He flew Mustangs in World War II. He won a lot of medals and came home a hero. After that, he studied at Purdue and became an electrical engineer." He looked at me as though waiting for a reaction.

"That's impressive," I said. "Does your dad still work as an engineer?"

"No, he died a few years ago."

Thomas seemed emotional when he said it.

"How did he die?" I asked.

"He died very suddenly. The doctors said it was his heart. He didn't really suffer at all."

I paused for a few moments, letting his words linger.

"Do you have any brothers or sisters?" I continued.

"No, well not now. I had a little sister who died of a birth defect a long time ago. It's really just my mother and me. I don't have any grandparents living, and my parents were only children."

I didn't say anything, and the waitress returned with our drinks.

He mentioned his sister again. "I was twelve when my sister died. She was six."

I didn't ask for the extra detail, and I didn't respond. I was unsure of what to say when he started talking again.

He went on to describe his sister and how her attitude was inspirational not only to him but to their whole family. When she died, her death was the only real setback in his life until his father's death eight years later. Thomas was anxious to tell me that as well.

Margery was home alone with Thomas at college when his father died. Thomas learned about the death from his football coach. It was just before the spring game, and the fans were both nervous and supportive of him as he missed the game. Thomas said the outpouring of sympathy was a great comfort to him. He also found some peace in the fact that his father never suffered and that his was a life well-lived and on his terms. It took his mother several months to pull herself together. Thomas continued with school, but in the early months after his father's death, he would come home at least twice a week to check on Margery. She gradually returned to the church and resumed her piano lessons, although most of her prior pupils had made other arrangements during her mourning period.

"It must have been a very hard time for you both," I said. It sounded weak to me when I said it.

"Yes, it was very hard. About the same time as Mom was starting to pull out, I was starting to crash."

"How do you mean?" I asked.

'Well, it started with withdrawing from my teammates and everyone around me. Then I couldn't sleep, and then I couldn't stop sleeping. About that time, I just couldn't stop crying. It was weird but terrifying."

I just sat with him while he said this.

"It was June and I was scheduled for summer classes, but I couldn't continue with them. I went back to the farm for the summer."

He was sharing with difficulty at this point.

"The worst part of all this was that Mom needed me, and I was no help to her. I think my dad would have been really disappointed with me."

"I'm sure you were a comfort to your mother," I offered.

"I don't think so," he said. "I think I was a drain on her. I should have been a better son."

I did not respond.

"It's all so fragile, isn't it?" he added. "You're here one day, and then you're gone."

When the food arrived, we spoke of less-weighty topics.

"Do you still follow the team?" I asked.

"A little bit, but it's not the same."

"Do you keep up with anyone from the team?"

"No, and none of the underclassmen I knew know that I came back to town. I don't want to see myself in the local paper as some sad human-interest story. You've seen those 'fall from grace' stories that are supposed to have a happy ending?"

"Yes, I think I know what you're talking about."

"Well my happy ending hasn't been written yet. I'm still looking for it."

"Aren't we all?"

"Cheers to that," he said, hoisting his water glass. "May we both find the happy ending."

I mentioned the old men in the bar to him, and his impression of them was the same as mine. They were four quirky old guys—well, three without Art—who were smart enough to band together early in life and lucky enough to have one another late in life. As much as they followed football, Thomas said, they never brought up the fact that he left the team, and he appreciated them for it.

We had coffee and then left. When I turned toward the car, he asked that we not go back right away and go for a walk; he started walking toward campus. We had covered almost a block before he started talking again. He seemed to just want to keep the mood going as we continued to walk. I listened while he made comments on the neighborhoods around us, of how this or that had changed since he first came to the university. He picked up his pace as we got closer to campus.

"How did you come to be a handyman at the Lafayette?" I asked.

"I wanted to come back to town, and they were advertising for the job in the newspaper. I could do everything they needed, and the pay was reasonable."

"How did you learn to do all the jobs you do for them?"

"Well, I grew up on the farm, and we did most of our own maintenance. My father was good at everything. Since I was about thirteen, we worked together. We rebuilt a few engines—both diesel and gas—on our tractor and a car I rebuilt from the bones. Over the years, we rewired our house and barn together. We remodeled the plumbing in our house, toilets, hot water heater—the works."

"That sounds complicated," I said.

"It wasn't complicated when I worked for Dad. The hard part was getting the finished product done to Mom's standards. She had me redo a few rooms, since her eye is certainly sharper than mine about those things. Anyway, Dad showed me how to do all of that stuff. I enjoy working with my hands."

"What kind of farming did you do?"

"We grew some feed corn for a while. We kept about a hundred pigs for about five years and then sold them off. Mostly we just grew grass or rented out acreage to some neighbors. My favorite crop, though, if you can call it that, was the apple orchard."

"I love apple orchards," I said, remembering some wonderful fall days in New York State.

"We have ten acres of apple trees. They were my dad's favorite, too. It was beauty in the spring and food in the fall. I loved growing up there and climbing in the trees. The irregular branches were great for climbing. The trees weren't that tall, and my parents never worried. I tried to name each tree when I was eight."

"Were they boys or girls?"

"That's funny you bring that up, because it was a puzzle to me. I didn't know what sex they were, and it took me a week to decide that I would give them girls' names since I knew more girls' names than boys' names. It took me another week to figure out that I didn't know that many girls' names either. When I grew tired of repeating the same name three or four times, I gave up. I eventually had two or three favorites, and I named just them. When I walk in the orchard these days, my two favorites are still there."

"What are their names?"

He smiled. "They're Margery and Jeanie. Margery is my mother. Jeanie was the sister I had who died."

The buildings of the campus were now in plain sight, and we walked toward them. He wanted to keep walking. He was quiet as we approached but kept a brisk pace.

As we stepped on the campus, he sighed a deep breath and said, "This is the first time I've been back here since I quit the team." He started to say something else but then stopped and waved a hand to disregard it.

He was nervous.

"Boy, I loved the game as a kid. Mom made me practice the piano as much as I practiced football. I hated the piano until I was about twelve. I wanted to be out playing the game. My father started throwing balls for me almost as early as I remember. I wanted to be there with him all the time. He was a quarterback in high school and taught me everything a receiver needed to do for his quarterback."

Thomas seemed to dwell on that as he looked ahead at the stadium. His pace slowed while he let it sink in.

"How did you keep up with your piano lessons?" I asked.

He smiled and then responded. "Dad was totally afraid of offending Mom, but if the truth were known, he didn't care whether or not I played piano. He and Mom did agree that neither of them wanted me to hurt my hands. But Mom certainly influenced me, too. I won a few competitions in the Chicago area, and my dad eventually liked the fact that I could play and that I would spend hours trying to memorize his favorite songs."

We were now in the shadow of the football stadium. He wanted to walk around the stadium rather than venturing further on the campus.

"I had some great times here," he said, mostly to himself. I said nothing but was attentive.

"It all started with the recruiting process, which is a complete flattery neurosis for a seventeen-year-old kid. I had forty scholarship offers for football, but I knew that I wanted to come here. I toyed with the idea of taking a few visits, but in the end, I didn't want to lead the other schools on."

He led us in a long walk around the stadium. It was as if he had conquered a small fear but didn't want to face a larger one yet.

"You seemed to love the game," I said. "Did you ever think of coming back to play?"

"No and actually, Julian, if it's okay with you, I'd rather not talk about any comebacks."

I started down another avenue with him.

"How long are you going to be the handyman at the hotel?"

"I don't know. Maybe forever," he said with a hint of a smile. "I don't really want to finish a degree. I'm not sure I want to do anything at home other than be a gentleman farmer. I don't know what direction I want to go with my music. It's cruel to be blessed with too many choices, and these days I can't think about much that's any further away than tomorrow."

Then he came back to remembering his playing. He started on his own.

"There's no bigger thrill in life than walking down that ramp on a Saturday afternoon. You're not just playing for the people in those seats; you're playing in front of a hundred years of tradition. You can feel it there, and whatever it is, it's pulling for you to win. It's weird, but it's real." Then he paused and added quietly, "I do miss that."

He lingered for a backward look at the stadium even as he led us toward the car.

Thomas came to the hotel early and met me at breakfast the next day. He wanted to talk more about his family and seemed to think I was a good listener. People came in the coffee shop just as he was warming up, and he seemed uncomfortable staying at the table when he was supposed to be checking the hotel punch list for maintenance items. He asked if I was available for another lunch the following day. It would be easier for him. I agreed, and we said we would meet at the same restaurant as before.

I went to the restaurant and waited, but he never showed up. I called him at work and was told that he had not come to work that day. He'd called in sick. I waited to see him at the hotel the next morning, but he didn't show again. On Saturday, I took a quick nap and shower after my shift. Then I went to see him.

His car was in front of his building, and I went upstairs to his apartment. I knocked loudly, but there was no response. I knocked again and called his name. This time, after a few moments, he came to the door.

"Oh, hi," he said with no enthusiasm to see me.

"Hi, yourself," I said. "How are you feeling?"

"Okay, I guess. Come in."

I followed him into the apartment.

"You didn't want to go to work this week?"

"No," he hesitated. "I just couldn't manage it. I didn't feel like being around anyone."

The shades were down, and the only light came from a single lamp. Even in the dim light it was obvious that his quarters were better than mine. He had one bedroom and a small kitchen, but his place was easily twice the size of mine. In his living room area stood a console piano with thick stacks of sheet music sitting on the lid.

I pointed at the piano. "Are you able to play here in the middle of the night?"

He shook his head. "No, the landlord said I could play only between noon and nine."

Scattered around the apartment were several family pictures taken at different times in his life. Most of them were pictures of the four of them. In one of them, his sister looked terribly frail. There were also photographs of his father standing next to his Mustang during World War II and of his parents at their wedding. Surprising to me somehow was all of the football memorabilia on display. There were multiple certificates, trophies, and sports photographs—some of teams and several action photographs of Thomas alone. Most striking was the display of his jersey framed and hung prominently on the wall.

He and I sat quietly. He seemed content to have me there, and I sat and waited for him to speak. Several minutes passed before he began.

He began haltingly before finding his stride. "Some days, I just kind of get blue and don't seem to have much interest in anything around me. I just don't have much of an interest showing up."

I nodded to show that I was listening.

"I'm not really lazy, but I have a hard time getting out the door. I needed a few quiet days, but I'm actually feeling much better today."

"Good," I said. "What was bothering you?"

"It was the same stuff that I worried about before. I'm not sure if I'm doing the right thing staying here."

"Where do you want to go?"

"I think sometimes I should be back on the farm helping Mom. She has encouraged me to get away, but it's hard. It would have been so different if my father had lived."

I let the comment hang there and waited to respond. "I know what you mean. I lost my mother to cancer when I was nineteen."

He was listening to me. I talked then about how many times I went back when she was hospitalized or when my dad needed me there for one reason or another.

"Did she suffer much?" he asked.

"Yes, a lot. But I always felt like my dad thought it was his tragedy and not hers. I spent more time helping him get along than helping her." I paused. "It wasn't a good time."

Thomas was quietly listening.

"I often think about how different my life would have been had she not been sick."

"I'm sorry for you," he said.

"Thanks," I said, and I meant it.

We sat for a while longer. After a time, he said, "Thank you for coming by. It means a lot that you came to check up on me." He stood, and I did also.

On my way out he stopped me. "I just want you to know," he said, "that I'll be there Monday morning."

He gave me a half smile and shut the door. He sounded sincere, and I did not doubt that he was coming back after the weekend.

On the following Tuesday, Thomas stopped by for coffee with me during my breakfast. His mood was much brighter, and he asked how I was doing, saying nothing about his concerns. I was just about ready to leave when he asked me, "Do you have any interest in coming home with me this weekend? I'm only going Saturday night. We'll leave here Saturday after lunch and be back Sunday afternoon. I have some chores to do on the farm, and I want to check in on Mom."

"Sure. I'd love to go with you." I was ready to get out of town and had even thought about taking a trip to Chicago myself. "It sounds great."

"I'll make you work a little, but my mother is a great cook; it'll be worth it."

"I look forward to it," I said, and I did. It was the focal point of my week.

CHAPTER 9

My workweek passed quickly. I did not check on Thomas, but I assumed that he had not been truant that week. He picked me up outside of my house a little before one o'clock on Saturday. For the first time since I had met him, Thomas appeared to have a sense of contentment. Although the football team was playing during our drive, neither of us wanted to listen to the radio broadcast.

The day was lovely, with a hint of fall in the air, and the foliage was only starting to exchange its green for the seasonal red, orange, and yellow. In the fifty miles we traveled to the farm, the land assumed a gentle roll. It was a landscape of plowed or fallow fields or of drying corn. The vista of the passing fields fringed in maples and elms against the backdrop of a cloudless bright sky made me wish the trip had been longer. It went all too fast for the beauty of the day.

The farm was on a quiet rural lane. The main house and outbuildings were set back about a hundred yards. Beyond them the apple orchard rose and fell. The home and barns were as picture perfect as any rural postcard scene. The barns were painted red, and as we came closer, it was clear that they were well maintained. The house was neatly painted, and the grey-blue clapboard finish was complemented by the sky behind and the fresh white porch in front.

As we approached from the road, a woman came out of the house and waved us in. A huge smile graced her gentle face. Thomas was home, and his face showed a new contentment as he returned her wave.

He eased the car down the long driveway and parked on the side of the house. The woman spryly descended the stairs to greet us. Thomas hugged her, and then she turned to me. Thomas started to introduce his mother as "Mrs.—" when she cut him off and told me to call her "Margery."

She led us indoors and asked us to sit with her in the living room. A magnificent oriental rug was the anchor of the elegant décor. The furniture was small in scale but fit perfectly. The only oversized piece was a full grand piano in the corner.

"How was your drive on this glorious day?" she asked me warmly.

"'Glorious' is the right word," I said. "The colors are just starting to come out." And then I added, "Your farm is just beautiful."

"Well, thank you," she said. "Thomas does a good job at keeping it up." She looked fondly across to Thomas.

Margery had prepared a pitcher of ice tea for us. We sat, and she asked Thomas about his work at the hotel. We made some further small talk about the trip, and then Margery asked Thomas what he was going to do around the farm. Thomas recited a full agenda, and she added a few small jobs in the house, which he was happy to do. After we finished our drinks, Thomas walked me to a back porch off the kitchen. There he pointed out the barns and the orchard and described the boundaries of their property.

"I'm going to change into work clothes," he told me.

"Do you need any help with anything?" I asked.

"No. You sit with Mom and get better acquainted. These jobs won't take too long."

Margery brightened with this and looked happy to have the company.

When Thomas left, she turned to me and smiled. "Tell me about yourself."

Ah, where to start, I thought. While Thomas was gone, we spent an hour covering all the basics. She pushed harder than I would have liked about my father's new family, and I felt a mix of sadness and guilt about expressing my feelings on the situation. She was easy to talk with and seemed to have a keen appetite for my mundane story. Her warmth made me miss my own mother. I don't know how much longer it would have gone on had Thomas not interrupted.

He returned with grease marks on his coveralls and matching stains on his forearms. Thomas waited for a lull in the conversation before asking if I wanted to take the tour. The question was posed like I expect St. Peter to ask about my first tour of heaven.

We walked to the barn. Parked outside was an old, nearly antique pickup truck. We loaded ourselves in the ancient truck and slowly moved out along the two-row dirt paths between the fields. Thomas and his mother owned most of a section plot. Except for forty acres that his father had sold to a neighbor ten years ago, they occupied the rest of the square mile. Thomas drove carefully, examining the land while he provided his narrative. The property had a fast-flowing creek coursing down one of the borders that fed a thirty-acre pond.

"Dad and I stocked this pond for three years with bass and baitfish," he said proudly.

"Are they still there?"

"Yes, and a lot bigger, now. I think the bass are pretty well established. We haven't stocked in about five years."

"Do you fish much?"

"Almost never," he said. "They're like pets now."

Thomas explained how the majority of their acreage was rented to neighbors and was now used for corn. Some of the fields were held fallow, and grass and other plants tried to settle in before the next planting cycle. Thomas pointed this out and was able to tell me both the common and Latin names of the weeds and the steps needed to control them when the money crops came back.

"We're coming to my favorite spot," he said as we drove into the apple orchard. The trees were full and ready for picking. He pointed out his named trees and described how he had spent most days of his boyhood in the orchard either climbing, pruning, or picking the trees or just walking between the rows.

"When I was in elementary school, my biggest fear was that these trees would come to life at night. I loved them during the day, but I was afraid to walk here after dark until high school."

Eventually, he brought us back to the barn where he garaged the truck. After parking, he pointed out the hog pens that were long vacant but still ready. Finally he led me to the barn's loft via a worn but substantial wooden ladder. From there, we could see over the orchard to the creek and the pond. I could see most of the farm spread below us.

"I used to spend hours up here," he said, almost to himself.

"It's beautiful," I told him. I was sincere. The late-day sun framed the outlines of the property and heightened the emerging early fall colors of the trees.

"I told you I had a little sister. I always wanted to bring her here to show her this view. She was always too weak to climb the ladder, and my parents didn't want me to carry her up." He paused as he reflected on this.

"I was twelve when Jeanie died, but I told her how magical this spot was and that it would always be waiting for her. I told her that when the doctors fixed her heart, we would come up here together and watch everything that happens on the farm. She always believed me."

He lingered for another moment or two and then ushered me down the ladder and back to the house.

Margery had tea ready for us. Just as Thomas sat down, he seemed to remember something urgent.

"I'm sorry," he said. "I forgot to relock the back gate. I want to do it before it gets dark. It'll take me about fifteen minutes." He smiled at me, saying, "You eat my share." Then he left.

His mother didn't protest, deferring to him on the urgency of tasks on the farm. "Hurry back" was all she said.

She poured tea for both of us and asked my impressions of the tour. After my compliments, she got to her point.

"How has Thomas seemed to you?" she asked.

"Oh, I guess he seems fine. We had a great tour."

"I mean back in town."

"He's all right, I guess. I think he feels down from time to time, but I suppose we all do."

She gently shook her head.

"I don't think we all feel like Thomas does," she said with concern.

I didn't respond.

"Well, I don't know how much of this he's shared with you, but Thomas has had some serious, uh ... nervous problems in the past."

"I didn't know."

"Well, I think he has it under control these days. Do you?"

"I suppose so," I said.

"Has he mentioned any sleeping problems to you?"

"Uh, not specifically, but I guess we all have sleeping problems sometimes."

"Not like Thomas, we don't," she said without hesitation. Then she asked, "Is he playing the piano?"

"Oh, yes. He's really talented, isn't he?"

"I'm glad he's playing. It does seem to keep him calmer." She thought a moment. "Yes, he is very good. I think he could have been quite a lot better if he had concentrated on piano, but that wasn't in the stars."

"He told me about being torn between piano and football."

"Yes, he was. James, his father, and I pulled at him constantly. He was just so good at music and at sports. We both had different visions for him. I knew that if he could pursue his music, he could do great things with it. James said that he could go to college on a football scholarship. But he was also good enough to pursue Juilliard if he had put his mind to it. I was his first piano teacher, but we sent him up to Chicago to study for several summers after he was eight years old. They wanted him to enter all of these competitions, but James wanted him back here on the farm. James won that battle, although I did manage to enter him into a few competitions outside of football season."

She looked out the window at the dropping sun. The shadows were stretching out in the room, and the air had become noticeably cooler.

She continued. "I suppose it was for the best. If I had forced him away from James, I would have been paralyzed with guilt now. Thomas just worshiped his father and would do anything for him."

"He still talks about that."

"Yes, he really idolized him. James was a fighter pilot in World War II. We married in Alabama during the war. James served in Europe, and I waited for him. He was going to be career military for a while. Near the end of the war, we moved up here to Indiana and he got out. Then he took a degree in engineering on the GI Bill.

I was happy the way it all turned out. I couldn't imagine myself being the wife of a career military man. I can tell you that in no uncertain terms."

She saw that I had finished my cup of tea. "Here, let me fix that for you." She poured another cup for me and then started her story again.

"At one time, James actually hoped Thomas would go to West Point. Now that was even farther from music than football. It was also about that time I backed off a little on his piano and let Thomas really devote himself to football. He was a tremendous athlete, and the colleges noticed. By the start of his junior year in high school, it was looking like we could save his college fund for graduate school. He eventually had scholarship offers from all over the country, but he wanted to stay close by. We were thrilled because of the school and because it was so close. He did well there … until James died in the spring of Thomas's sophomore year. James had enough warnings about his heart, but he ignored them all. He died in his sleep. I still remember his laugh that night before he turned out our light."

She slowly shook her head and stopped her story. I didn't have anything to say. For a minute or so, we both listened to the ticking of the mantle clock in the quiet of the room.

Then she spoke again. "Have you met the girl he's seeing, Danielle?"

"I've met her," I said. "I don't know her well."

"Well, she's made a big impression on Thomas; I know that."

"She's beautiful."

"Yes, that's what Thomas says." She chose her words carefully. "I hope she understands that Thomas can be complicated. He can be difficult sometimes."

"I really don't know," I said lamely.

"I just want him to find himself and to be comfortable with what he finds. I don't know what he wants to do. I know he's smart and talented in many ways. I hope he at least goes back to school to finish that degree. After that, he has so many options. I do wish James were here to help him."

With that, we heard Thomas climbing the porch steps.

"What a great day, right?" he said to no one in particular as he entered.

We sat and listened as Thomas gave Margery a rundown on the maintenance issues with the farm. Most of the jobs were minor and he had already dealt with them. A few more were parked on his list for his next visit. One or two needed some outside help, but he would arrange all of that for her. He asked his mother if she had invited the neighbors to pick apples that year. She said she had but was more selective about whom she asked on the property these days. She didn't want too many strangers.

Thomas brought out two bottles of beer for us, and Margery brought out some modest hors d'oeuvres. They all disappeared in a few minutes. After the second plate and the second round of drinks, Margery put her arm around Thomas and asked him to play a duet with her. He gladly agreed. I listened for the next half hour while they played several four-hand pieces they had obviously played before. Even so, it was clear that each of them loved to improvise a unique sound where classical and jazz blended effortlessly. When they tired of playing together, they each took turns entertaining the other with brief selections.

Thomas left to shower before supper, and Margery excused herself to the kitchen. I also went to my room to change before dinner. Despite any intentions I had to help Thomas with his chores around the farm, the only work I managed was my climb up to the loft. Still, I felt the need to clean up. I had the impression that Margery would want that even if she didn't say it.

When we returned, Margery had herself changed clothes and had set a lovely table with candles and wine. She sat Thomas and me at the ends of the table and took a seat between us. The dinner was simple but elegant, and the next several hours passed quickly with the retelling of several of Thomas's experiences from his first piano recital to the last college football game his father saw. A few bottles of wine vanished during this time.

"Mom, do you remember the Mozart competition in St. Louis?"

"Oh Thomas, you shouldn't tell that story," she said with a smile that spoke to a false objection.

Thomas ignored his mother and looked at me. "The short version of the story is that I had played pretty well, and it was near the end of the competition. I was followed by just one other player. He was a little guy, about half my size, and he wore thick Coke-bottle glasses. He was wearing a suit three sizes too big for him. You hated to laugh at him, but it was hard not to."

Margery was looking on and shaking her head slowly.

Thomas continued, "Well, this kid played his heart out, and he was just perfect. The judges thought he was the best in the competition, and even I agreed with them." He started to laugh. "I shouldn't laugh," he said, "but when the winner was announced, this guy stood in front of the auditorium to accept his trophy. He tried to thank the judges, but he had such a terrible stutter; he couldn't even get 'thank you' out of his mouth."

"It was a sad scene," added Margery.

"The only reason it was funny was the way the kid looked and the fact that he had just mopped up the competition with his playing. Well, then the most amazing thing happened. He dragged the microphone over to the piano bench and started talking while he played. He spoke flawlessly. He thanked everyone from his parents to his teacher to the judges and lots of other people as well."

"He thanked the Lord too," said Margery.

"Yes, he did," confirmed Thomas. He paused to take a drink and then continued.

"Well, they couldn't shut him up. Eventually they had to take the microphone from him. He got the longest standing ovation I have ever heard. I wish someone had filmed it. I'd watch it every day."

"That's a great story," I said.

"I wonder what happened to that young man," asked Margery. "I'll bet that's an interesting story too."

Margery stood and with that comment started to clear. She directed the cleanup, and it went quickly. When the kitchen was back in order, she announced that she was going to bed. Thomas kissed her good night, and we sat comfortably in the living room as she ascended the steps.

"What did you and Mom talk about while I was out today?" he asked after Margery had disappeared into her room.

"Well, first she wanted to hear about me. Then she wanted to hear about you."

"She knows all about me. Did you volunteer any of your dark past from Binghamton, New York?"

"I slipped open my vault just a hair, but most of the really bad stuff stayed buried."

"Good, good," he said and took another sip of wine.

"It's interesting how you won your mother over to football."

"More Dad than me."

We'd both had a lot to drink, and I couldn't master my curiosity or my tongue.

"Tell me again why you gave it up," I said.

He paused and then locked eyes with me. "I never told you the first time."

"You're right. You never told me."

"I have the feeling that you're going to keep asking until I tell you." He was serious and seemed a little sad about the reality of the situation.

"I'm sorry; it's just that I—" He cut me off.

"Don't explain. I'll tell you." I felt guilty but was expectant. I sat quietly.

He paused to collect himself and then started speaking.

"It happened after my father died. I felt a huge burden because Mom couldn't stop crying for about two months. I missed most of spring practice. I didn't come back to school for the summer and missed the first two weeks of August camp. Coach understood and didn't hold it against me. I managed to come back in September, since Mom was doing much better. I started classes and started practicing and tried to get back in the rhythm around there. I was able to play myself back into the starting lineup and had some good games. Then I started going strong, like nothing could stop me. I remember a few great weeks, but then it all seemed to unravel again. I was struggling to keep it all together, and I was panicking because I was losing the fight and I knew it. On the outside, I'm sure it looked like my life was normal again. Inside, nothing could have been further from the truth."

He drank some more. I filled my glass and probed a little.

"It sounds like you were holding up pretty well, given all the expectations that were on you."

"I wish that had been true," he responded. "I felt like the world was closing in on me. I didn't know the person I was becoming. Everything I was doing was wrong for me, or so I thought at the time. I didn't belong. I barely said a word to any of my teammates. They assumed that I was just in some kind of grieving cycle, and they left me alone. I would wake up each day with crying spells and memories of Dad. I didn't feel like playing, but I kept going through the motions because I thought Dad would have wanted it. I was only doing it because I guess I felt somehow obliged to his memory. It was a huge effort to stay motivated."

"It sounds like it was very hard. Was Margery able to help you then?"

He shrugged his shoulders and said, "Mom was doing the best she could, and even though she was better, she wasn't ready for crowds. She didn't come to any of the games, and when I was on the big stage, I was on my own."

He stood and began to slowly pace the floor.

"In my head, the clouds became darker and darker. I went home one Sunday. It was about three in the afternoon, and Mom was napping. I went to the bureau where I knew Dad kept a gun. I told myself that it was for Mom's benefit not to have the gun around at that time, but I don't think that was the reason I took it. I took the bullets too. I brought them back to school with me."

He paced faster now.

"Wow," I said. "What were you thinking?"

"I wasn't thinking; I was feeling, and it wasn't good. It continued to worsen for me emotionally. I felt like I was such a millstone to anyone who was forced to be around me. The world could be a better place if they didn't have to deal with me anymore. All I could think about was the gun."

"Didn't you talk with your coach or seek some counseling?" I asked.

"No. I didn't talk with anyone about it. When you're that low, you just don't feel worthy enough to share your troubles with anyone else."

He sat down across from me and took a deep breath.

"I kept thinking like that for a few weeks. Soon, though, it all started to unravel. I would miss a practice and come up with some reason for doing it. Then I was benched for missing too many practices. It kept getting worse. I was almost thrown off the team for missing a game. I didn't know what to do. I couldn't perform anymore. I went home, and I remember that I just hid in the barn for the day. Eventually I went in the house and cried with Mom. Mom called Coach the next day, and it was only because of her that I didn't get tossed off the team."

He paused.

"I was tired of letting the world down. I had let the team down. I had let Coach down. I knew I would have disappointed Dad. The worst was how I felt I was a terrible burden to Mom. I didn't even think of the fans. I thought of everyone being better off without me ... and I thought of the gun. After awhile, it wasn't me anymore. It was me in a movie, and I didn't like what I was watching."

He turned away from me and lowered his eyes before starting again.

"The day it happened was a rainy cold November morning. I couldn't sleep. I had been awake all night. I finally went out for a walk on campus; I didn't know what I needed or wanted just then, but I took the gun with me. I walked around crying. I didn't see another soul; I was completely alone. A little before dawn, I made my way over to the locker room. I found one of the security people who recognized me. I told him I had left some books in my locker, and he let me in."

Thomas paused for much longer this time.

"I sat in front of my locker for what seemed to be hours, but nothing in my world seemed real. It was quiet. I thought of Dad, and Mom, and my sister. I cried and imagined how much better off Mom would be without me. I felt shame. I had let her down when I should have been helping her. Then it changed, and again it was like I wasn't there. I barely remember the details of the rest. When I pulled out the gun, it didn't feel like it was me doing it. I do remember thinking it was really loaded. Then I stuck it in my mouth and was about to pull the trigger."

Thomas now looked me full in the eye; he was crying.

"Just at that moment, Coach walked in and saw me. He had left something there the night before and wanted to have it before he started his workday. I guess I should be glad that he works almost all the time during the season or I wouldn't be here today. When he came in the room, we both froze. Then I lowered the gun and handed it to him, and I started to cry."

Thomas stood again, slowly pacing and seemingly reliving the scene in his head.

"Coach also had tears in his eyes as he sat with me. He hugged me and wouldn't let me go. Coach and Mom managed to get me into a hospital and on some medication. The university was discreet, and I went quietly away. After I was discharged from the hospital, I saw a psychiatrist who did me a lot of good for about a year. I see him occasionally now."

Thomas shook his head and quietly added, "I really screwed up. I disappointed my mother, and it was a terrible legacy to leave for my dad."

Thomas looked away from me and continued to cry. I sat quietly for a few minutes.

Then he sat again and looked at me. "I guess I'm telling you because you're the first person to ask me about it since I got it straight in my head what happened."

We sat for a few more minutes while he composed himself.

He then stood and gently patted me on the shoulder. "I'll see you in the morning," he said and left me there to ponder the story.

CHAPTER 10

I rose in the morning greeted by the smells of bacon and coffee. It was the home I wish I still had. I dressed quickly and went to the kitchen. Margery was alone cooking. Bach organ music was on the record player. The sound filled the room, and she didn't hear me until I was right next to her. She explained that Thomas had risen early and was already working in the barn. With the aromas from the kitchen, I was in no rush to join him.

I had a delightful breakfast with Margery. We did not discuss Thomas. Instead the conversation centered on the farm and how she had learned to cope without James when Thomas was not around. She had three renters, and they were all from contiguous properties. Two of them paid her cash, and the other provided maintenance work, adjusted for the yield of his crop. She and James had been leasing out the extra land for a few years, and she was happy about it.

"Thomas seems to love it here," I said.

"Yes, he does."

"Do you think he'll come back and be a farmer?"

She laughed at this. "He loves everything about farming except the dirt."

"What do you mean?" I asked.

'Well, we both like to see the crops grow, but Thomas has no interest in either putting them in the ground or taking them out of it."

We finished breakfast. After cleaning up, I relaxed at the kitchen table reading a newspaper. Margery sat in the living room and read her Bible. She told me that she had arranged for a substitute organist at the church. We both looked up as we heard Thomas cross the threshold. He walked behind me and placed a hand on my shoulder. Margery looked up but seemed to have expected that we would not be staying until the afternoon. She then continued to read while I went upstairs to pack.

Thomas was subdued on the drive back. It was another beautiful day, and it seemed like the leaves had changed their colors overnight. The land gently rose and flowed from one horizon to another and then slowly flattened as we drove north. Thomas seemed fully immersed in thought, but after a half hour of driving, he became interested in talking again. Eventually he made it around to asking me what he really wanted to know.

"After our conversation last night, do you feel any different about me?"

I was half expecting the question.

"No, but I feel good that you could share that with me. It must have been awful."

He nodded as he watched the road.

Then I added, "If you ever need to talk, I'm here to listen. Also, I want you to know that I'll never tell anyone about that conversation. It's your story to tell. You can trust me."

"Thanks. I think I have a good handle on myself these days. I feel great now. Nothing's going to slow me down."

"Good," I said, but I wasn't convinced.

After a few minutes I asked him, "Does Danielle know your story?"

"No, she doesn't." He looked uncomfortable telling me this.

"Are you going to tell her?"

"Sometime for sure, but I don't think I can bring it up to her now. Like you, she just wants to know that everything is under control—and it is."

We both quietly sat and watched the country slide by. *How many people*, I thought, *just stay out here and live peaceful, perfect lives?* How many are happily unaware of all the mess in the world? How many just grow their crops and raise their hogs and forget about all the other issues of the outside world? Were they happier for the insulation, the illusion, or did it all catch up with them in the end? Then I thought of James, Margery, Jeanie, and Thomas and answered my own question.

"Will you be going to the Algonquin this week?" he asked.

"I imagine I'll go see the old guys at least once. You know, you threw off their whole schedule with your concert."

He smiled. "I know; they gave me an earful after they switched nights."

"Art's doing all right, though."

"Art's always going to do all right. The only thing he's going to lose money on is the Lafayette."

I was confused. "You mean he owns the Lafayette and the Algonquin?"

"Yes, and about half of the rest of the town as well. Art's a rich man. All he wants to do in life, though, is play cards with his friends."

"It sounds like he does take care of his friends," I said.

"He does," agreed Thomas. "He loves all the attention people give him. He makes me laugh as he sits back in that booth like it's a throne."

We watched a few more farms pass, and he asked me what I thought of Danielle.

"I hardly know her, Thomas. My impression is that in addition to being pretty, she has a great personality and is one of the great attractions for Art's bar."

After a few moments, Thomas said, "You two had a long talk last week, right?"

"Well, a short talk, actually."

"What did you talk about?"

"Well, truth be told, she wanted to know how I thought you were doing. She was concerned about you."

"Was she upset that I wasn't sleeping again?"

"Yes, that was the gist of it."

"What did you say?"

"I told her that you woke me up in the middle of the night with your piano and that you looked unnaturally good the next morning. I didn't tell her that it was an amazing concert or that I was exhausted the next day."

"That's it?"

"Yes, that covers it."

"Sometimes I get a little wound up. It's not dangerous or anything. I feel good when I get that energy. I feel like I can do anything. It's just the opposite of being depressed. I wished I had that kind of energy more often. Playing balances me and helps me relax."

"If you can show me how you get that energy, please do. I could use it sometimes."

We drove on a while longer, and he was quiet.

"But you and Danielle are friends," he said.

"I guess," I said.

He continued, "You know she's trying to save money. She wants to go to nursing school when she has enough saved."

"How long have you been going out with her?"

"We've been dating for about five months now. We started dating about a month after I came back."

"How serious is it?"

"Oh, I think she's going to be the one. I really do. I've never met anyone who makes me feel like she can."

"Congratulations," I said.

He smiled.

"I have a question," I said. "What about the big guy, Eddie? What did you do to rile him? He doesn't seem to like you very much."

Thomas shook his head as he answered. "Eddie's a jerk. He was two years ahead of me in high school. He grew up right here in town. He was a good football player. We played his school every year. We always beat them in football, although they usually won in basketball." Thomas paused as if savoring the memory.

Then he continued, "When I was a sophomore, I was named to some of the same All-State teams as he was as a senior. He went to Michigan State on a football scholarship as a tight end. In his first year there, he put on a lot of weight and they switched his position to tackle, but he never worked hard to increase his strength and was a big disappointment. He said he hurt his knee and that's why they made the switch, but I think it was just that he ate and drank himself out of being a tight end. The word was that he liked drinking beer more than he liked playing football. I heard they took his scholarship away when he was caught driving drunk around campus. I guess he's jealous of me. At least I was able to play for a couple of years. For some reason, he blames me for his stupidity. I don't understand it. But you're right. He doesn't like me."

We were approaching the outskirts of town now.

Thomas turned away from the road leading to my house. He said that he had to pick up some things at his place. He would be seeing

Danielle later, and he needed a change of clothes. We picked up his things, and then he dropped me off at my place.

I had agreed to work another Sunday night, and after Thomas dropped me off, I went into work early and parked in the hotel lot. The sunny day was now surrendering to the autumn dusk, but I found it hard to retire indoors. I crossed the street from the hotel and walked over the bridge spanning the river. The revetment walls on either side of the river had been constructed in the twenties but were modernized and fortified. They rose about twenty feet above the water, ready to deal with any flood surge. On the far side of the river, the wall dissolved as a parapet to a riverfront footpath that led to a city park. I walked the path to the park and back, encountering one or two neighborhood kids with long cane poles, hoping to entice a carp on this lovely autumn day.

From the river's edge, the Lafayette looked stately and prosperous. I thought that Art must have made this walk many times in hopes that it would be as it appeared. The scene was peaceful and serene, with sparse traffic on a late Sunday afternoon. I thought of others my age on the other side of the world and felt lucky to be there as I watched the sun die beyond the city's modest skyline.

As I went in to work, I found it hard to imagine a gifted young athlete ready to kill himself. I remember that it felt good to be alive that afternoon.

CHAPTER 11

The crispness in the early October air continued after our weekend at the farm. The cool air and the bright sunshine were both cleansing and uplifting. I was in fine spirits. My classes were going reasonably well, considering that I had, to some degree, deprioritized them. I was comfortable at work, and I had already submitted several graduate school applications. Life felt pretty good, and it wasn't just me. The weather had worked its wonders on everyone at the Lafayette that day. The town and the hotel all seemed to have been planted in a new happy place.

When I entered the lobby, I was surprised to hear the piano. It was not Thomas's usual day or hour for entertainment. The music was lively, with ragtime and popular tunes. I stopped briefly in the bar and then made my way into the great room of the lobby. It was indeed Thomas who was playing. He was still in his work clothes.

The day man had called up to Mrs. Howard, and she rushed right down to listen. She was not as put together as she was during her Wednesday appearances but certainly more than when I would bring her dinner. Granger had apparently not felt the trip downstairs worthwhile as he was nowhere in sight. Mrs. Howard, however, was flanked by the working girls, Eileen and Sherlene, and they were all giving their full attention to Thomas. Marco was not there. Without him, the girls looked relaxed and almost wholesome. The three women sat together thoroughly enjoying the music, and Thomas seemed to feed off their spirited support.

Out of the corner of my eye, I watched Art descend from the mezzanine. He had a smile on his face as well. Max walked in during the second or third piece Thomas played, and the day man spoke to him briefly and walked out. I had nothing more pressing than to claim a sausage sandwich in the kitchen. The food would be there whenever I needed it, and I just sat and listened while Thomas entertained.

He played for the better part of an hour, and no one left. He announced the title of each piece before and after playing it. Over time, several guests moved closer to his piano. Eileen and Sherlene moved aside to help accommodate them, even though Mrs. Howard refused to budge from her spot. Although Thomas was not entertaining requests, the crowd spoke as if with one voice in favor of the up-tempo pieces. It was that kind of day.

When he finished, Mrs. Howard hugged him and thanked him. The hookers faded into the crowd, and Marco appeared on cue. The three went to the bar. A few of the other guests complimented Thomas, and one of them, a new arrival, asked him if he was a piano tuner by trade.

As the crowd dissolved, Thomas came over and said, "Danielle and I are going to try to get away to Chicago this weekend. Hey, what did you think of the music?"

I started to answer, but he asked, "What did the hookers think? Did Mrs. Howard like it? Did Art stop by?"

He couldn't stand still while he waited for me to answer.

"Hey, look, I gotta go." Then he turned and walked away.

"It was great talking with you, Thomas," I said to his retreating back.

As I watched him hurry out the front door, I thought, *He's flying high. He's heading for a crash.*

The girls emerged from the bar about an hour later. The younger of them, Eileen, or Lemon Top to Ernie and Ben, looked bored.

"How are you tonight, Mr. Night Bellman?" she asked.

"I'm doing well," I responded, and I meant it.

"You go to the college, right?"

"Yes, I do."

"I was thinking of going to college."

"What would you like to study?"

"I'm not sure; maybe psychology. I think I have a pretty good idea about how people think."

"That sounds interesting."

She paused, not wanting to leave but looking not quite comfortable with staying.

"You probably have a pretty low opinion of me, don't you?"

"Well, I don't have any opinion, really. Anyway, why would you care?"

She thought about that. "I don't know," she said and then made for the waiting elevator car. Before entering it, she turned and said, "Your friend, Thomas, is amazing, isn't he?" She turned without a response, and the elevator door closed behind her.

I stopped in the now-empty bar to listen to the evening news. It was nothing new. The body count numbers were encouraging, but the newsman in the rice paddy sounded less than optimistic. It wasn't clear why. I couldn't listen to it any longer, and that may have been the point.

The rest of the week was quiet. I had no plans for the weekend and went to the Algonquin late in the afternoon on Saturday. I had agreed to work another overnight shift with the weekend man if I could start about midnight. He had big plans for the next morning and wanted to be fresh. The usual Algonquin patrons were at the bar.

Eddie was with his pal, engaged in an animated conversation. Walt, the foundry worker, was sitting under the TV quietly watching the game. Horace, a retired custodian, was in the corner with his head in the newspaper. Next to him and sharing his newspaper was Mike, who had been a bank teller and who was rumored to have been fired for some unknown "irregularity" in the cash tally one day.

Art was not there, and I was conscripted to the card table by the three professors. It was a big football game for the team, and the three were more interested in the television than in the cards. After a few hands, the men put their cards down. It was in the final quarter of the game, and they all wanted to concentrate on the outcome.

"How are your studies going, young man?" asked Pete during a time-out.

"Oh, I suppose they're going. It's only a couple more months until I'm done," I answered with little excitement.

Ernie looked at me severely. "'Carpe diem,' and that means every 'diem.' Remember, as the philosopher says, 'Nothing great was ever achieved without enthusiasm.'"

Pete nodded and added gravely, "And the preacher says, 'For whatsoever a man soweth, that shall he also reap.' Sow a little happiness for yourself these days. You will not be a young man forever."

Ben added, "And the poet noted that 'to me, every hour of the light and dark is a miracle.'"

They each were pleased with themselves for producing an appropriate quotation, and they waited for me to respond. I didn't, so they filled the space.

"To be young again; how sweet would that be?" asked Pete to the table.

"Peter, as our resident professional theologian, you of all of us have your sights on the 'terminus ultimus,'" said Ben. "How shall we guide this young man?"

Peter looked at the others. "It's a complicated business giving advice, especially to the young. Maybe we're too old to advise."

"The philosopher teaches the following," said Ernie. "The older you get, the older you want to get."

"I'm not sure I agree," said Ben. "Sometimes I agree with the poet who says, 'Nothing can happen more beautiful than death.'"

I remembered Thomas's experiences and kept my thoughts to myself.

"Well, back to you, young scholar," said Peter.

"Yes?"

"How will you make it through this, er ... brooding egocentric phase of your extended adolescence with a little more gusto?"

"One day at a time and with renewed enthusiasm," I said, picking up on their theme.

"Good. It's important to do more than just gadding about with us. Live it. This life matters for the next one," said Peter.

"'Be, and not seem.' So says the philosopher," chimed in Ernie.

At that time, Art arrived. They greeted him and told him it had been painful to suffer my play since I had not yet acquired the skill to play cards and watch football simultaneously.

Art apologized for being late. He had seen a business partner for a late-afternoon meeting.

"As the philosopher says, Arthur, 'Money often costs too much,'" said Ernie sternly.

Art shook his head at him. They continued their banter and game and did not comment as I stood to leave.

I was walking out while Danielle was walking in.

"Hi," she said as she saw me at the entrance. "I'm just picking up a sweater I left here. Thomas and I are going out."

"You didn't go to Chicago."

"No, something came up."

"Is he coming in?"

"He's just parking the car."

"Good, I'll wait to say hello."

All eyes were on her while she walked to the kitchen. She was dressed for an evening out and looked spectacular.

A moment later, Thomas came in the door. He looked around the room and waved at Art and the professors. He was dressed in a jacket and tie.

"It looks like you're planning a big night," I remarked, sizing him up.

"Dinner and a movie," he said with a smile. "No trip to Chicago."

"I heard."

Thomas was standing near the door with his back to the bar. I noticed Eddie and his friend rising to leave. Eddie had been listening to our conversation.

As he walked by, he pushed Thomas in the back with his huge forearm, shoving him hard. Thomas never saw it. The force of the blow nearly lifted him in the air. He banged into the wall and landed on the floor. Eddie stood over him waiting for Thomas to react.

"Excuse me," said Eddie. "You were blocking the door." Thomas simply glared up at him from the floor. Eddie then turned to his friend. "Hey, the All-Star goes down pretty easy, doesn't he?" Eddie laughed.

When Thomas moved to regain his feet Eddie reached over and pushed his shoulder. Thomas hit the floor again.

"Stay down there, peanut. I'm just leaving."

Eddie turned away, and as he started outside, Thomas regained his feet and started after him.

Thomas moved toward Eddie, but Danielle's voice rang out firm and clear. She must have watched the scene from across the room.

"Thomas, don't!" she said. Thomas hesitated and turned to her. His face showed a rage I had never seen in him. He took another step toward the door.

"Don't!" she repeated. He stopped. "Come back here and we'll talk." She walked to him and took his hand. She spoke to him quietly for a moment and then led him to an empty booth near the kitchen. No one interrupted them. She spoke. He listened.

I went back to the bar where I heard the old men commenting.

"You should ban that oaf from this place," Ben told Art.

"He's a pestilence," said Ernie.

"Be not deceived; evil communications corrupt good manners," added Peter. "And that's from the preacher himself."

Art took a second to look at each of them. He thought a moment more and then said. "Thanks for the advice, gentlemen. Just young bucks locking horns is how I see it. Let's move on. Whose deal is it?" Art did not want to engage further.

I ordered a beer and nursed it until Thomas and Danielle left. Then I had another. I was a few hours early for my shift. I paid up and took a walk on down Main Street. People were out, and the city showed some life in her.

I crossed the river on the bridge and looked at the reflections of the city lights in the black water. The buildings, street lights, and traffic signals were all reflected faithfully on the river. The only exception was that the traffic signals showed neither green nor yellow nor red in reflection. The river made the lights whatever color you wanted them. I waited there for a few minutes and then crossed back to the hotel.

The weekend bellman had just made a tobacco run for Granger and was returning to the lobby. I told him to go home early and enjoy his day tomorrow. I found food in the kitchen and made a dinner of sorts. I didn't have time to eat it until almost midnight, as the requests for room service and the check-ins kept coming.

After my dinner, the bar announced last call, and the one or two stragglers returned to their rooms, their homes, or some other late-night spot. By one o'clock, the lobby was quiet. I brought a textbook for one of my courses and made good progress with it until two thirty, when I put it down and tried to sleep.

At about four, I woke to the sound of the piano. Thomas was playing, and the music was somber. Had I been sleeping much farther from the piano, the music would have been a great inducement for my sleep.

As it was, I listened to him play but still tried to keep my eyes closed. I was not completely successful. He kept going for about an hour. At last he stopped and walked over to me. My eyes were open, and I watched him approach.

"I'm sorry about tonight," he said. He seemed a little drunk.

"Sorry for what?" I asked. He was mumbling and standing a little unsteady.

"For that stuff across the street earlier. I probably could have handled it better."

"How? By going after him when your girlfriend begs you not to? That wouldn't have taken you very far."

"I don't know. Maybe by not being there, I could have avoided all of it."

"Sure, and maybe if Eddie hadn't forearmed you in the back, he could have avoided it too."

"Yeah, I guess." He paused and then continued, "Well, Danielle calmed me down and we had a nice dinner."

He rose to leave. I asked, "What happened with Chicago? I thought it was going to be a big weekend."

He shrugged his shoulders and started to walk out.

"It fell apart," he said over his shoulder.

"Why was that?" I asked as he walked further away.

He slurred, but I thought I heard it correctly when he answered, "She had babysitter problems."

CHAPTER 12

As the fall progressed and I thought ahead to my uncertain future, I felt ever more detached from college life. I was not exactly in love with the Hotel Lafayette or my colleagues either. I didn't feel bonded with the campus, the hotel, or the town. It was unsettling, but Ernie's critical assessment of my current "joie de vive" was spot on target. It was a sense of apathy not just for friends or memories but also for what each day would bring. In a funny way, I did not feel alone in this. I think many people my age were somewhat adrift during those times. Country, cause, and self were three concepts that chafed ever more uncomfortably against one another. For most of the day's causes, the campus community could reliably provide an affirming chorus. But that didn't ring true anymore for me. The only "-ism" that captured me was cynicism. It was a good time to be a committed cynic, and perhaps that is why Thomas took me into his confidence. He needed a jaundiced eye that he could trust.

October's peak of color did bring out the best of the campus before it surrendered to the inevitable winter dormancy. The lakes were ringed with myriad hues of brown, red, yellow, and orange as the trees reached their final crescendo before the season's act closed. As the leaves began to fall, the campus had ever more "radicals" in our midst to raise our awareness. I didn't worry too much about them, though. I was growing up, and they were just a different form of entertainment until I left. Besides, my awareness was assaulted each time I looked at a television.

I don't know how much of my lack of engagement was due to the fact that the US military had already rejected me for future employment. At the end of my semester off, I was called in for an army induction physical. The army doctors weren't happy with how the accident had affected my vision. The idea of being labeled damaged goods at such a tender age was painful to my ego, but I recovered rapidly as I watched so many of my friends receive their draft notifications. The uncertainty of what the next several years would hold for me seemed a small price to pay for the certainty of knowing what I would not be doing. So I had no real worries. Like most of my generation, I could continue to embrace my comfort. I could try to stay interested without having to become involved.

After Thomas's melancholy concert, I didn't see him for a few days. Then he called and asked me if I wanted to meet him for coffee. He suggested coming by his place late in the afternoon and we would go from there.

His apartment was neater than before, and the reams of sheet music on the piano lid had been removed. There were fresh flowers in the kitchen. I sat on the piano bench. When I looked in his bedroom as he was changing out of his work khakis, I noticed some women's clothes hanging in the open closet.

"How is it going with you and Danielle?" I asked.

He smiled widely. "It couldn't be better." And he continued to change.

"Did you tell me that your trip to Chicago was canceled because of 'babysitter problems'?"

"Did I tell you that? I was kind of ... well ... overserved on Saturday, but that's what happened."

"Who is the baby?"

He paused. "Oh, I thought you knew. It's Danielle's little girl. She's really not a baby. She's nine. I thought you knew that."

"How would I know? I had no idea."

"I thought someone would have told you—like the old men across the street."

"No, they're more in a teaching mode than a gossip mode when I sit with them. Except for Art, the other three just love to compete with one another to see how many 'learned' quotations they can fit into a conversation."

"Yes, they used to do that with me too. They never tell you who they're quoting. They want to make you work."

"I know Peter is quoting St. Paul. I think Ernie is quoting Emerson. I really don't know who Ben is channeling."

"Peter is taking it easy on you. With me it was Aquinas and then St. Augustine. By the way, he still calls me Didymus and I call him Cephas. Ernie loves Emerson, so that's probably right. With Ben, it's probably Whitman. He loves Sandburg, Frost, and Whitman. But with Frost and Sandburg, you probably would have recognized at least some of the verses."

"How long does this go on?"

"Until they run out of lines. With them, that could be a long time. It was four months for me. Be warned, though; they may switch to another source to make it go longer."

"Anyway, they said nothing about Danielle or her daughter."

"Well, she has a kid, and that was the problem with the Chicago trip. Danielle's mother usually watches her, but she had a better offer that night. She canceled on us at the last minute." He finished changing and walked from his bedroom. "Let's go."

"So what was the better offer?"

"I have no idea, but not much would surprise me. Her mom's life is a series of failures—three marriages, lots of good-for-nothing boyfriends, can't keep a job."

I didn't know what to say. Finally I said, "That surprises me. Danielle seems so responsible."

"Food stamps and Danielle's tips keep her mom in cigarettes and TV dinners."

"What about her dad?"

"Her mom has his identity narrowed down to three possible guys. All worthless. When I marry Danielle, I hope we can stay away from her mom as much as possible."

Over the next few days, I replayed this conversation frequently in my mind. I wondered how vulnerable Thomas would be if this relationship went badly. There was also the lingering image of the gun and the locker room and his hidden disgrace.

Thomas also wanted to tell me that he had been back to the Algonquin twice since the incident with Eddie. The first time, he sat down and had a good visit with Art while he was waiting for Danielle to complete her shift. Art told him he saw the whole event unfold, and he agreed that Eddie was the offending party. Thomas's next time back to the Algonquin was last night. Eddie was there, and he was reasonably sober. He apologized to Thomas for the earlier incident. Thomas said he accepted the apology and thought no more about it. He said he let it go completely.

After coffee, I drove by the Algonquin and the hotel. I felt no urge to stop at either place. The campus was alive, but I continued to feel more distant as the semester passed. I retired to my apartment; as humble as it was, it felt like a sanctuary.

The next morning during my post-shift breakfast, Thomas parked himself at my table. He was excited because he and Danielle had rescheduled their Chicago trip for the next weekend. He had not taken her to the farm yet. It didn't appear that he was planning to in the foreseeable future.

The rest of the week passed without event. Thomas gave his Wednesday concert and did not come to play during my precious sleep in the middle of the night. I did not see him or Danielle on Saturday when I went to see the four card players and to hear some obscure quotations laced between words I had never heard before. It was a quiet day in the Algonquin. The team was playing away. The game was a laugher and was essentially decided in the first quarter. With the outcome never in doubt, the card play went faster and the quotes flew easily. I was not working, so I treated myself to a few additional beers. I was going to a party near campus that night, and I actually felt collegiate once again.

I woke the next morning, surprisingly not too much the worse for the wear. I had left the party earlier and more sober than I predicted I would. It was another beautiful autumn day, and I thought of driving up to Chicago myself. Thomas and Danielle had put me in the mood. I had not been to the museums or walked along the lake since before the accident, and I had planned to go before the end of the semester. Just as I made up my mind to go, Thomas called me.

They had just returned. Danielle had to relieve her mother from babysitting as the woman had suddenly acquired a pressing social obligation for the afternoon. They drove back to Indiana early that morning. Thomas had had such a wonderful time with Danielle; he had to share it with someone. He wondered whether we could meet for a late lunch.

My half-formed plans were no match for his enthusiasm. I agreed to meet him for lunch, although given Thomas's complicated emotional history, I didn't want to walk too deeply into the weeds of his love life. Being his confidante sounded like it might include a responsibility I could not manage. I also thought it something of a "girlfriend" thing that the other gender did and I should strive to avoid. Nevertheless, I arrived at the lunch spot at one o'clock as agreed.

When he still hadn't arrived at almost one thirty, I decided to leave. But as I stood to go, he walked in.

"I'm sorry I'm late," he said with considerably less energy than he'd shared on the telephone earlier.

I looked up but said nothing. I wasn't angry. I just had nothing to say.

He continued with his explanation. "We had an argument, and it was a longer call than I expected." He said it as though that was the final word on the topic.

"Are we still having lunch? I'm starving," I said.

"Sure, sure," he said, not looking at me as he picked up his menu.

Neither of us said anything again until after ordering.

"Well, how was Chicago?" I asked, trying to bring us back on track.

"It was great. We had a good meal, went to some bars, heard some music. It was a good time." His voice did not ring with the earlier gusto. He seemed to have completely lost interest in discussing his trip.

He didn't come back to the trip during the meal. I didn't either. We engaged in sports talk, although he was obviously not that interested. He seemed preoccupied with something.

At the end of the meal, he told me he was meeting Danielle at three that afternoon to take her daughter to a park. I knew the park. It was next to a high-end shopping mall, and I had driven by there several times. I was finishing my coffee as he abruptly rose to leave. As we parted, he told me, without much emotion, that he appreciated me coming to lunch with him. He said he would try to come to work early one day next week and we would have breakfast together. He also encouraged me to come to the Wednesday recital as he was preparing a long selection of Mrs. Howard's favorites. He patted me on the shoulder and left.

After another cup of coffee, I went back to my apartment for an hour and then made an excuse for myself to buy a toy for my half-sister's coming birthday. I went to the mall near the park Thomas had mentioned. I could not understand why I wanted to be the voyeur on their relationship, but I needed to see the three of them. Perhaps it wasn't just a "girlfriend" thing after all.

When I arrived, they were in the playground area. I parked the car a discreet distance away and tried to read their body language. The weather was cool, bordering on cold, and there was only one little girl on the swings. She appeared to be about nine years old. Danielle and Thomas were locked in a conversation that looked neither friendly nor pleasant. I watched for a minute or so as the body language went from bad to worse. I had seen enough, and I left them to buy my gift. I prepared myself for some late-night piano visitations in the coming week.

CHAPTER 13

The next day, after spying on their family outing the day before, I was curious about Danielle's mood. I went to the Algonquin for a late lunch when I knew she would be working. Except for weekends, I had never been there at this hour of the day. Two regulars, Horace and Mike, shared a newspaper while they ate their lunches. I didn't recognize the other lunch patrons. The bartender was also a new face to me. I learned that Art platooned his bartenders from a crew of six men. These men all had a long history with Art and had worked for him in one capacity or another for years. They were all friendly but professionally detached and did not spend much time listening to the patrons and never dispensed advice.

Patrons who were looking for a soft, sympathetic ear had to rely on the waitresses. In addition to Danielle, Art employed two girls who worked a later overlapping shift and another who worked days when Danielle was off. Of all of them, Danielle was the favorite, and not just because she was the most attractive. She was by far the most friendly and the most skilled at making a patron feel special in a one-minute conversation.

Art was in his usual booth. Ernie was with him. It was not a regular day for the other card players.

I waved to Art and Ernie and sat at the bar a few stools down from Horace. He looked up to say hello and then went back to his reading. Mike did not look up.

I ordered a drink from the bartender and asked him to send Danielle over for my lunch order.

"Hi. I saw you came in. How have you been?" she asked.

"Good. How was Chicago?"

"It was fun. I had to cut it short, but it was fun." I didn't think she meant it.

She took my order. Then she hesitated and quietly said to me, "Can you stick around after you finish lunch so we can talk during my break?"

I told her I would.

Horace was not much for conversation, but he let me borrow their newspaper. After I finished lunch, I caught Danielle's eye. She told the bartender she was going out for about a half hour and asked him to cover for her.

She grabbed her coat and left the bar. I paid my tab and followed her out.

She was waiting for me about twenty paces from the door. She started walking as soon as she saw me and did not stop until she crossed over the bridge. Together, we took the stairs down to the footpath.

I smiled as I came to her. "Well, tell me about Chicago."

She thought about her answer. "It really was fun." Then she thought for a moment. "You know there's nothing quite like going into a piano bar with Thomas, especially if he's been drinking."

Curious, I waited for her to explain why.

"What happens is that when the piano bar player eventually gets ready to go on a break, Thomas talks him into letting him sit at the piano. Thomas studied in Chicago and can do some name dropping,

111

so they know he's not going to get up there and do 'Chopsticks' or something stupid.

"Well, he sits down and starts something classical and then switches to jazz and then to songs that everybody hums. Then he gets everyone to clap in time to the music. By then the piano bar piano player comes back. After the crowd has heard Thomas play, it sounds like he doesn't really know how to play the piano. Then Thomas goes over to him and whispers something in his ear and they play together, and it sounds a lot better than the poor guy playing alone. By the time they're done we don't have to buy any more drinks and the whole bar wants to be Thomas's friend."

She looked past me, smiling at the memory.

"We went to three piano bars, and the result was always the same. By the time we hit the last place—we were both a little drunk by then—Thomas only played classical music, and although people were impressed, it was kind of heavy and we didn't get as many free drinks." She looked up to me. "But people were truly impressed."

We walked a little further. The weather was extremely cold for the end of October, and worse forecasts were on the way. She flipped her coat collar up as we faced the wind.

"So you had a great time?" I prompted.

She thought and then answered slowly. "We did, up to a point."

"What do you mean?"

She took another breath.

"The only reason I'm telling you this is that you know him and he seems to trust you."

"Go ahead. I'm listening."

She hesitated but then said, "I think Thomas is a lot of fun. He's a brilliant musician, and he can be very sweet."

"I agree."

"Well, he can also be temperamental at times. There are nights when he just talks so fast and just wants to get his point out. He won't listen. He argues with people. He won't sleep and doesn't understand that sometimes I can't keep up with him. He gets angry. Sometimes he's impossible to be around."

"I know he has come to the hotel in the middle of the night to play piano because he can't sleep."

"Yeah, that's right. I have been with him at the hotel when he's done that, but not since you've been working there."

"How long has this been going on?" I asked.

"At least five or six months, the whole time we've been dating." Then she added, "You know, he's never mentioned it, but I think that's why he stopped playing football. I think he picked a fight with one of his teammates or his coach and got himself thrown off the team. I bet he threw his whole career away because he couldn't manage his temper."

I said nothing but just kept listening to her.

She continued. "He's got another problem too. He kind of drops out of sight sometimes, and he won't call or even answer the phone for days at a time. When I ask him about it, he just says that either he was at the farm or needed some alone time."

I nodded, waiting.

"You know, he's just high-strung and difficult sometimes."

"But you have fun with him."

"Yes, we have fun, a lot of the time."

"Then what's wrong?"

She didn't answer right away but slowed her pace.

"I have a lot going on in my life now. I'm sure you know I have a daughter. She's nine years old, and she's my number-one priority."

"And Thomas has a problem with that?" I asked.

"Oh no, Thomas adores her."

"How does she feel ... What is her name?"

113

"Jenny."

"How does Jenny feel about Thomas?"

"She's crazy about him."

"And so what's the problem?"

"Thomas is the problem," she said definitively. "If we were just going out and having fun, that would be great. That's easy, and we both know what we're getting out of it. But he wants to take the relationship to a different level."

"What do you mean, get married?"

"Yes."

"Did he ask you?"

"No, but I know he's going to."

"And you don't want to get married."

"No. I think I'm a sucker for athletes. I fell for one when I was in high school, and I don't want to do it again. I worked my tail off to get my diploma after Jenny was born. My mother is a loose cannon, and my child-care situation was never any good. Having someone take care of me sounds nice, but the reality is that I'll end up taking care of all of them. I don't see Thomas as being all that stable."

I listened but made no comment.

"Look, Thomas is a great guy. But he lost something when he dropped out of school. Right now, I think he just wants to prove something to himself before he moves back to that farm. I don't think he's really thought any further than that. I think the big picture for him is to live on the farm and take care of his mother."

"I don't know," I told her truthfully. "I've never asked him what his big picture is."

We walked a little further.

"What about you?" I asked. "What's your goal in life?"

"Me? I just want to get out of this town and do something other than what I'm doing now. I've lived here all my life, and I'm ready to move on."

"Why don't you go?"

"Hey, I'm saving up my money to do just that."

"Thomas told me you wanted to go to nursing school."

"First I get out of here. Then I'll figure out the rest of it. I've been a waitress for three years, and I'm tired of it. I'm tired of the job. I'm tired of the people. I would have been gone a year ago if Art hadn't been such a great boss."

"Where would you go?"

"I'm not sure, but I know I don't want to go live on his farm. I want to go someplace warm."

"It's a beautiful farm."

"I don't care."

I waited for her, but she remained quiet.

"Have you met his mother?"

She shook her head. "He's tried to get me out there, but I haven't wanted to go."

"What if Thomas would move with you? What if he'd go south or out west?"

She didn't hesitate. "No. It wouldn't work. I couldn't be married to him."

I said nothing as we walked back toward the bridge.

"Don't get me wrong," she continued. "I think he's a great guy, a little strange perhaps, but a great guy. He's smart and funny, and most of the time I like being with him. But I don't see it going forever."

I was becoming uncomfortable with the conversation. I probably should have stopped it several minutes before. We didn't speak as we scaled the steps from the path back up the bridge. When we reached the top platform, I asked the payoff question.

"Danielle, why are you really sharing all this with me?"

"Because he trusts you."

"So?"

"I want you to talk to Thomas."

"And say what? That he's difficult? That you don't think he's stable? What do you want me to say?"

"I don't know," she said. "I was hoping you could figure out a way to let him know in a way that wouldn't hurt him."

"Danielle, if he's set on asking you to marry him and you're set on saying 'no,' then there's no way his feelings are not going to be hurt." My voice sounded harsher than I had intended.

She said nothing as we walked across the bridge and walked down the street to the Algonquin.

"I guess you're right," she said as we came back to the door. "It won't be easy. I think it will kill him when I tell him."

CHAPTER 14

There was no sign of Thomas over the next week. I couldn't pretend that I cared, and I even made it a point to miss the Wednesday concert. I was finding my courses a little boring and, frankly, did a lot of daydreaming about what shape my future would take after graduation. I also had several papers to write and a test to take. It was relatively easy to put Thomas and Danielle out of my mind.

That time of year did not help. My mother had died at the end of October, and since she died I couldn't help but dwell on the memories during that anniversary week. When the leaves started falling, it brought it all back.

Still, the week passed quickly, and although boring, my course load was demanding. On Saturday morning, I treated myself to a very large breakfast after my shift. I had very little additional schoolwork to do that weekend, and I was loitering in the coffee shop reading. I was on my third newspaper when the weekend relief bellman came to find me.

"Hey, Julian, you got a phone call at the front desk."

"Who wants me?" I asked.

"Someone called 'Margery' or 'Margie' or something like that."

I left my table and walked to the office behind the front desk.

"Hello, this is Julian."

"Julian, this is Margery. I've been looking for Thomas and can't find him. I've called a few times this week and he wasn't at home. Do you know where I can reach him?"

"No, not really, I haven't seen him," I said without much enthusiasm. "Is there a problem?"

"No. I just wanted to check in with him to make sure he's doing all right. I just had the need to hear his voice."

"I'm sorry, Margery. I haven't seen him all week."

She paused and responded to something she heard in my voice.

"How are you doing?"

I didn't know if she really wanted the true assessment or the watered-down version. I shaded my answer to the former flavor.

"I guess I'm all right. I just find that I get a little down this time of year. It's when my mom died. It was four years ago, yesterday."

"I can hear it in your voice, Julian."

"It will pass pretty soon. I'll be fine."

She hesitated and then asked. "How would you like to drive over for a good meal today? We can have an early supper and you'll still make it back at a decent hour. I think you can use a little company."

I thought about it and decided I couldn't tell her "no."

"Margery, thank you. What time do you want to see me?"

"Let's say four o'clock. And if you do see Thomas, bring him along."

"That's very nice of you, Margery. Can I bring anything else besides Thomas?"

"Julian, just try to bring a smile."

"I will."

"I'll see you then. Good-bye."

I felt better already. Her voice was comforting, and her concern was genuine. I had missed that for the last few years.

The trip went faster than I had anticipated, and the drive on that beautiful day was the first truly pleasurable experience I'd had all week.

When I drove down the driveway into the farm, there was no sign of life. I parked my car in front of the house, and as I walked up the front porch steps, I saw an apple-picking basket with a note in it.

The note was to me from Margery. She said that an older neighbor needed her to drive her into town but that she would be back a little after four. She asked if I would mind collecting a basket full of apples from the orchard. She assured me that our pie was already made and that these apples would be used to create a cobbler for her church group later in the week.

I strapped on the basket and walked to the carefully planted orchard. The trees were well laid in straight rows but showed their individuality in the irregularity of their branches. The trees looked well tended and seemed to have no urgent need of additional pruning. The apple leaves were multicolored but thinning and aging with the season. Most of the trees were heavy with fruit, as Margery had indeed limited the traffic in the orchard that fall. Apples dangled from their stems in the light breeze, almost begging me to take them. I loved being there, and I saw no one else on this perfect autumn day.

At about the same time I filled my basket with my carefully selected harvest, I heard a car coming down the lane. I looked over as Margery left the car and waved to me before she went in the house. I finished my basket and walked down the hill to join her.

I walked to the house and entered the back door. Margery was in the kitchen as I entered, and she flashed a big smile. She came over and kissed me on the cheek.

"It's good to see you, Julian. Did you hear anything from Thomas?"

"No, sorry."

"That's okay. We'll have a good visit. I have beer and wine. Wash up, make yourself a drink, and relax in the parlor. I have a few things to put in the oven. I'll join you in a few minutes. Thanks for collecting the apples. It looks like you picked some good ones."

I smiled at her and washed my hands. I opened a bottle of wine and went to their living room with the plate of cheese and crackers she put out. She was just a few minutes and then joined me.

"How are you feeling now?" she asked.

"Better, I think. It's hard to be down when you have a day as pretty as this."

"Yes, it is."

Then we sat until she said, "Tell me about your mom."

Then I did. I told Margery everything. I told her about the ovarian cancer and the treatments and how sick they made her. I told her about Mom's denial up until the very end and then how stubborn she was that something as trivial as her death would not stop me from going to college.

"That was the hardest for me," I told her. "I wanted to be with her at the end."

"You did what she asked of you," she said.

"Yes," I said. "I always did. She didn't want me to see her when she was so sick. But it was worse for me not seeing her."

Margery sat quietly.

"Then, when she finally passed, I flew home from college alone. We buried her, and then my dad expected me to take care of him. He was a mess, but I quickly grew tired of him."

"Why was that?"

"He wasn't grieving for Mom. He was feeling sorry for himself. He never saw how I felt."

"I'm sure you're wrong," said Margery.

"I don't know," I muttered. "I just felt so alone. I went back to school because I promised Mom I would, but I really just needed to get away."

Eventually I started to cry and told her how very alone I had felt for a long time, not just since my father remarried but throughout Mom's entire illness when she would not let me be a part of it. She would not let me say "good-bye." I composed myself and then continued.

"It wasn't more than five months later that Dad told me he was dating Barbara. I couldn't believe it."

"Some men need to rush right back into relationships," she said.

"I'm sure they were already living together when he called me. I didn't get angry, but I think he heard my disappointment with him."

I paused, remembering how I felt.

"At least they waited a year until they married. It was a year and a week actually. I came back for the wedding but left as quickly as I could. I know he was hurt by me, but I didn't care."

Then, without even being aware of when it started, I started to cry uncontrollably. I don't know how long I did cry, but I remember repeating, "I just feel so alone."

She let me say that for some time, and then she held me by my shoulders.

"Julian, you are not alone. Believe me; I will always be here when you need me."

And I did. And she was.

The meal was wonderful, and Margery continued to be incredibly supportive to me. She was very understanding about my seasonal declines and gave me good counsel that this too would pass. She ended the meal and my short psychotherapy session with apple pie and ice cream. She was right, at least in predicting the magnitude of those moods over time. I would never stop dreading the end of October, but I could live with it if I remembered that it was also apple season. I didn't think of Thomas again until I returned to town.

CHAPTER 15

It stayed unusually cold through the cusp of November. Except for the rare oak, the trees were long bare. Stripped of leaves, the rocking branches whispered to the cruelty of a gelid wind those first days of the dark season. I was never a fan of winter. Hibernation was entirely logical to me. I wanted to go to ground as soon as the cold snap hit. Also, since I was really just marking time now in my last full month of college, sleeping for the rest of the semester sounded like a wonderful idea.

The heating system at the Lafayette worked well, but the creaking and snapping of the lobby radiators broke the peace of the deep nights during those first frozen days. I had not seen Thomas in days, not since Danielle confided in me.

It was a busy night. The girls were staying in. According to Eileen, there had been some problem at the motel out by the airport where they were working and they were waiting for things to "settle," as she put it. I brought dinners to their rooms. Sherlene and Marco needed more to drink, so I made another delivery upstairs with a bottle from the bar.

Granger needed cigarettes. When I took care of that, he asked me in and poured me a drink before I could say no. I stayed to talk with him for fifteen minutes but was finally able to remove myself and retreat to the lobby.

I returned to the lobby a little before nine. Max was waiting for me, and he told me to remove a tattered old man from the sitting area. The squatter was dirty and frail, looking all the smaller as he was swaddled in a ripped and stained greatcoat several sizes too large for him. He sat on the floor in the far corner of the lobby, leaving the chairs open for any paying customers. I wanted to plead the man's case with Max, but I knew that would go nowhere.

The old man's face was sunken on both sides, but one side was further dented, and his eye wandered on that side. His deep blue eyes were vivid, outlined in a bloodshot field. His hands were bones wrapped in parchment. He could not stop fidgeting with his overly long sleeves, continuously pulling them over his hands. His expression was detached and dreamy but peaceful. As I approached, he looked up and focused on the hand I extended to him.

"You have to leave," I told him.

"It's cold," he said in a soft voice.

"I know."

He looked at me still not moving.

I looked back at Max, who was watching intently. Then Max pointed to the door. The man and I both watched Max.

"Mister, you have to go. He'll call the police."

"It's cold," he repeated in a louder voice.

I looked back at Max, who was shaking his head.

"You have to go now."

The hobo looked at me for what seemed like an hour and then asked me to help him to his feet. When he stood, he was unsteady. I piloted him around the circular door and felt the shock of the cold air as I pushed him out.

Max was back to his work by the time I returned to the lobby. He said nothing, and I assumed that this would become standard operating procedure until spring. I was glad that I would miss most of the winter at the Lafayette.

Around ten o'clock, I was thinking of settling into one of the wing chairs with some textbooks I'd brought along. I was also still thinking about my conversation with Danielle and wondering how that was going to play out. Just when I pulled out my book, Max called me over.

"Did you bring Mrs. Howard her dinner tonight?" he asked.

I hadn't thought of Mrs. Howard with the evening's other distractions. Although Mrs. Howard occasionally ate late, this was very unusual.

"No," I answered. "Are you sure she's in?"

"She's in," replied Max. "Go check on her and make sure she's okay."

I reluctantly lifted myself out of the chair and was starting toward the elevator when Max waved me back.

"Take a pass key," he said, holding one out.

I felt uneasy about this errand as I rode the elevator to her floor. I was even more concerned when I knocked and there was no answer. I knocked again and then went to the end of the hall to call Max on the house phone. He told me to go into her unit and find out what was going on.

I feared the worst.

I knocked once more, waited, and then pulled out the key and unlocked the door. Her lights were off, and I fumbled around for a minute to find the switch for the lights.

When the lights came on, I nearly jumped out of my skin. She was sitting in a chair at the small table where she took her meals. Her chin was resting on her chest. Her eyes were opened, and she was dressed. I spoke to her, half-expecting a response. None came.

I called her name again. Still no response, no movement. I recovered from my surprise and walked to her. I touched her hand.

It was cold. Other than my own mother at her wake, Mrs. Howard was the first dead person I had ever seen. After my initial shock, I remember being full of curiosity. I must have just stared at her for a minute or two before I called Max for further instructions.

Max told me to wait in the room while he arranged for the bartender to watch the front desk. He promised to come up in a few minutes. While I waited, I walked around the apartment, now taking in details I had never before noticed. Each of her photographs must have been forty years old. There were no photographs of her with anyone who seemed to have a reasonable chance of still being alive. Her cupboard was well stocked with cereal and other staples, and I think she was planning on being alive to consume them. There were no pills or empty bottles in her bathroom, and I thought that the idea of suicide was remote. Other than going though her drawers, which I decided not to do, that was all the information I would get. She actually looked remarkably good, all things considered.

Max arrived with Art in tow. He had come from the Algonquin as soon as Max called him. They carefully inspected Mrs. Howard before they were willing to believe she was dead. When they confirmed my diagnosis, Art assumed command. He called the police and an ambulance company. He then called Hal and briefed him on the situation. He then excused himself, and ten minutes later the police and ambulance arrived. A few minutes after this, Art returned to her apartment with a folder of papers. By now, Granger had heard the commotion in the hallway. He entered the apartment, saw Mrs. Howard, and then left, looking like he was going to cry. He lit a cigarette in the hallway and then quietly drifted back to his own place, overwhelmed by the flurry of activity around Mrs. Howard's unit.

Art rummaged through the folder he carried and was able to provide the policeman with the name of Mrs. Howard's next of kin, a niece in Chicago. After the police informed the niece, Art said he would follow up with another call to her. Apparently Mrs. Howard had left explicit instructions for this eventuality, and Art wanted to confirm the acceptability of her directives with the niece in the morning.

The police and ambulance people were efficient and soon conducted Mrs. Howard out of the Lafayette for the last time. The policeman ordered Art to keep the door locked on the room until the medical examiner had ruled out any foul play. Art said that he wanted to take one thing from the room before they sealed it. Mrs. Howard had specified a burial dress in the folder, and the policeman allowed me to look for it with Art's direction. The officer watched while I went to her closet to recover the dress. Max took it and said he would hold it behind the lobby desk for the funeral director when the time came. Then, with a flourish, we all left. The door was locked, and that was the end of Mrs. Howard's stay at the Lafayette.

Art returned to the Algonquin before I had a chance to speak with him. Max went right back to work. I felt unsettled and thought for a moment that I should go up and see Granger and comfort him. I didn't, because I didn't know what to say. I went back to the lobby and went about the routine chores for the rest of the night. It passed quickly.

I waited for Thomas's arrival the next morning. I wanted to tell him about Mrs. Howard myself. Thomas came in at his usual hour.

"What is it?" he asked when he saw me.

"I'm sorry to tell you this, but Mrs. Howard died last night."

He took a few moments to let it sink in.

His gaze was tracking all around the room.

I told him the whole story, including how sudden it must have been; that she did not look at all like she suffered. I let him know that Art was managing the family and that the funeral arrangements would be forthcoming later in the day or tomorrow. I wasn't sure he was listening to me. He was either indifferent or just not processing this.

He thanked me for telling him. I thought it was a formal and uncaring thanks. His only other comment was "She was a nice lady." Then he walked off.

The niece worked long hours, and she wanted to speak with someone in the evening if Art could arrange it. Art decided I should be the point person to orchestrate the funeral service with the family. I had some misgivings about this, but as it happened, there was no family other than the niece. There were also no friends the niece could locate.

The time and place of the ceremony were posted at the Lafayette, and I made sure I taped a copy over Thomas's locker. I did not see him after the initial announcement.

The service was to be simple, without a specific funeral liturgy. Mrs. Howard wanted a casket and a graveside service but no church ceremony. The medical examiner was able to release Mrs. Howard's body within twenty-four hours, and the funeral parlor would be ready to stage Mrs. Howard's prescribed ritual a day later. With my help and the help of the funeral parlor, the niece arranged for a small plot in a local cemetery.

Were it up to the niece, even this degree of memorial was too much. She was a spinster and the last bud surviving on the family tree. Mrs. Howard had been the youngest of six siblings. She was born outside of Chicago in a farming community, an area that would now be considered a near suburb. Mrs. Howard's sister, the niece's mother, had died of cancer about twenty years before. She had four brothers who all went west, and they were all childless. One of them died in World War II in the Pacific, and the others died of more-or-less natural causes over the last twenty-five years. Mrs. Howard had no children and had been a widow for almost forty years. Her husband was an only child. She was eighty-nine when she died. The niece was about sixty.

I called Thomas after the funeral announcement came out but received no reply. I waited for him on the morning of the service, but he didn't come to work.

I was in the lobby looking for Thomas just before leaving for the service when Eileen appeared. I almost didn't recognize her. She was dressed in a conservative skirt suit, and her hair was pulled back. She looked quite attractive. She wanted to go to Mrs. Howard's service and asked if I would drive her. She had no car, as she usually relied on Marco for her transportation needs. We waited a few more minutes, hoping to catch Thomas, but we never saw him.

The cemetery was about fifteen minutes from the hotel. When we arrived, the casket was mounted on the frame above the hole next to a single enormous flower arrangement that Art had provided. I met the niece just before the ceremony and introduced her to Eileen, whom I think she initially mistook as my date. In addition to those two, Art and Peter were also there. They were talking with the funeral director, who seemed both interested and relieved to hear that Peter was a priest. He asked Peter if he would mind saying a few prayers over the gravesite after Art had volunteered to give modest eulogy. When Peter agreed, the funeral director went to find warm shelter in his car until the extemporaneous service concluded.

The five of us stood awkwardly around the casket shivering and not sure of where the service's starting line should be. Finally, Art spoke. Mrs. Howard had lived in the Lafayette for seven years. He had known her for the last five, which was when he became involved with the hotel. He spoke of her kindness and of how much she loved the piano music the hotel offered. He spoke of how dear she was to the hotel staff. Then he abruptly ran out of steam. He asked if there were any others who wanted to speak, and he looked at the niece. She smiled and told the group that she didn't really know her aunt well since her mother never really spoke with her sister. She did add that she had wished she had known her better and that Mrs. Howard and her mother had been closer. That was all the niece could contribute.

Art then looked around the little circle again and asked if there were other comments before Peter would lead us in a final prayer. Art was looking hard at me for a contribution, and I searched for the right platitudes.

Just as I was about to spout a few clichés, to our collective surprise, Eileen addressed the group. She talked about how she and Mrs. Howard were very close and they would often have breakfast together. She shared a number of stories as one would of their favorite grandmother. She went on for about five minutes and then turned to Peter and asked him to bring Mrs. Howard home to the Lord. Peter did just that.

Afterward, Art took us all out for a lunch. None of us except Eileen had much in the way of personalized remembrances at lunch. Art ordered some wine and talked to us about what a curse it is to live too long. To outlive your friends and spouse, or God forbid, your children was not worth it. Not only do you have to wait and watch them die, but when you go, there won't be anyone left to come to your service.

Mrs. Howard's niece became interested in Eileen and asked at the table what she did for a living. Initially, Eileen pretended not to hear, but the question was repeated loudly. I think it was a wonderful credit to the three of us that we did not change our expression when Eileen told her that she was a "hostess" in the "hospitality business."

After lunch, Art and Peter drove the niece back to the train station. Eileen touched my hand as they left and asked me if I would do her one more favor. I said I would. She asked me to take her to the hotel where her suitcase was packed and then bring her to the bus station. She was going back to southern Indiana. I drove her to catch her bus, and that was the last time I ever saw her.

CHAPTER 16

It was the Friday after the funeral, and I still had not seen Thomas. For days, I waited around until his shift started and tried to catch him during the day, but he was either late or missing. I wanted to talk with him about Mrs. Howard and try to understand how her death might have affected him. I called his apartment several times during the week without a response. I even drove by late in the afternoon, but he wasn't in, his car wasn't there, and there was no answer at his door. So I was a little surprised that he called me at the hotel that Saturday morning after I finished my Friday night shift.

He wanted to meet me for dinner. Danielle had agreed to cover the dinner shift for one of the other waitresses and would be working a little later at the Algonquin. Thomas was free, and he wanted to see me. More importantly, he said he had some exciting news to share with me.

In prior conversations, we had discussed his future. He knew it was my strong view, also held by Margery, that he should finish his degree. I hoped he would tell me that he had reenrolled at the university and the reason he had been such an elusive target during the prior week was because he was making these arrangements. I prepared a congratulatory speech emphasizing how happy this would make his mother. I wondered whether his rematriculation was a possible outcome of a conversation Danielle may have had with him.

I arrived at the Algonquin about four o'clock. The crowd was mixed between the evening crew and the sports crowd from the afternoon. Most of them were engrossed in the football game on the television. Mike and Horace were there, but the other regulars weren't around. Art wasn't there, and neither were the other old men. I wondered if their Algonquin routine was only a three-season hobby and whether any of them were snowbirds and had already gone south.

Danielle saw me and smiled stiffly. I assumed that she was not happy with me for declining to be the bearer of the bad news in their relationship. She was hopping a few tables, and I was enjoying my second beer. I saw her slow down and stop in the corner by the kitchen. I went to speak with her. She almost turned away from me as I walked up.

"How are you today?" I asked, trying to take her temperature with a pleasant opening.

"I'm okay," she said blandly.

"I haven't seen Thomas this week. How is he?"

"No different," she said.

"Have you two had that conversation you were thinking of?"

"No."

I was a little surprised.

"Are you going to?"

"I don't know." Then she stepped into the kitchen and said to me as she left, "Look, I have to go."

She went into the kitchen, and I had the clear impression that she would not be coming out until I left. I thought of ordering a third beer just to see how long she would stay in there. Then I thought better of it, settled my tab, and went over to the hotel to kill the time before dinner with Thomas. There wasn't much going on at the Lafayette, so I just sat in the lobby and read a newspaper.

When I reached the restaurant, I was delighted to find that Thomas's mood was the opposite of Danielle's. Initially, I was delighted. Thomas had never greeted me with such a joyful smile. I was at first relieved, but then as we talked, I started to rethink the feeling and my misgivings took charge.

Thomas was higher than I had ever seen him. I could not keep up with the conversation, and he had no patience waiting for me to hold up my end of it. He asked me hurriedly about Mrs. Howard's funeral and then went on to the next topic before I could answer. He had something else on his mind.

When the waitress came over, he ordered two beers for himself and his dinner. I was still looking for a menu, but the waitress fortunately did not abandon me and I ordered from memory.

"Where have you been keeping yourself the last week?" I asked.

Thomas ignored my question and instead asked me, "I'll bet you're wondering what my 'big news' is."

"Yes, I am," I said, deliberately trying to slow his pace.

"I just heard some exciting information."

"About school?" I probed.

"No, about Danielle," he said proudly.

"Oh, what about Danielle?" I knew that this was not going to turn out well.

"I don't want you to tell anyone," he said.

"What is it?"

"Well, she's pregnant, and we're getting married."

"Say that again," I said, hoping I had not actually heard it.

"She's pregnant, and I'm going to marry her."

"Really?" This wasn't adding up. "When did you learn?"

"Oh, she called me earlier today. She just found out. She's so excited and so happy," he said almost breathlessly.

I now had a terrible feeling about this, and the feeling worsened as he continued his high-energy monologue.

"I just know that Danielle, Jenny, and the baby will all love the farm, and Margery will love having us. I wonder how Margery will get along with Danielle's mother. What do you think?"

He didn't wait for an answer.

"You know there might be some friction with all of us right away, but those things work out. When do you think I should tell everyone at the hotel about this?"

While he continued to muse about his future with Danielle, the drinks and food came. I had little appetite. I ate slowly while he continued to natter away about the perfect situation life had presented to him. It was a bubble that was going to burst, but I was not the person to do it. He wouldn't have heard me anyway.

I asked him, "What will you do when you get married; I mean, work-wise?"

"Well, I think I'll be a real farmer and play music on the side," he said.

"Thomas, even your mother says you don't like farming. Do you really want to do that?"

"Yes, of course I do," he said quickly. "I love the farm. I've thought a great deal about it. First we'll bring back the pigs. I'll want to expand the orchard over time. Then I'll have to get a tractor—I think I can find a used one to rebuild. I know how to grow corn and soybeans, and I know I can make a living out of this if I supplement it with my music. I think both Danielle and Jenny will love the farm, don't you?"

And so it went for the rest of the meal. It was all so positive, but nothing approached reality. He rushed through his food and then insisted he had to leave. I was only half finished with my plate when he popped up and abruptly excused himself.

"I have to run," he said. "I have some things to do before I pick up Danielle at the Algonquin at ten. Maybe I'll see you later. Thanks for dinner." Then he tossed a wad of bills on the table and almost ran out of the restaurant.

I leisurely finished my meal alone as I watched him cross the street and nearly jog down the block.

I had time on my hands with Thomas's sudden departure. Campus was quiet on the weekend before Thanksgiving, and there was nothing to do there. Given my light course load, I was not really academically overwhelmed. I went back to the hotel to collect my paycheck for the week, which was held at the desk.

When I arrived at the hotel, the weekend desk clerk handed me a note. It was a message to call Margery at the farm as soon as I could.

I walked down to the private office and made the call.

She answered on the second ring.

"Hello, Margery," I said. "It's Julian. How are you?"

"Julian, have you seen Thomas?" she asked with no small talk. There was worry in her voice.

"Yes, I just had dinner with him," I said, trying to sound reassuring.

"Do you know if he's taking his medicine? I know it's an odd question, but I thought you might know."

This was a question I had not expected. "No, Margery. I don't know anything about that."

"Well, he called me, and he doesn't sound right. How did he seem to you?"

"I think he seemed ... distracted."

She waited a few moments before responding. "Please have him call me when you see him."

"I'd be happy to," I said. "Is there anything specific that you want me to tell him?"

"Thanks, no. Just have him call me."

"I will."

"Before I hang up," she added, "did Thomas invite you for Thanksgiving dinner?"

"No, he didn't."

"Well, he should have. Can you come?"

I was dreading staying around campus or eating at the hotel on Thanksgiving. Hal had offered me the day off if I wanted to switch with the usual weekend bellman.

"I'd love to come," I said.

"Good. I look forward to seeing you. Julian, please have Thomas call me when you see him, okay?"

I assured her that I would.

CHAPTER 17

After Margery's call, I sat in the lobby of the hotel watching the traffic outside through the large street-facing windows. The weather, already ugly with sleet and wind, was worsening with the sleet changing to snow and the wind picking up speed. Snow was beginning to collect on the sidewalks and parked cars. I was happy that I was going to miss the winter season here. It was getting off to an ominous start.

The weekend bellman and I were reasonably friendly with one another. I found him accommodating about changing shifts. He didn't have much going on in his life except the hotel and was easily swayed to accept another shift. Fortunately, he didn't mind working on Thanksgiving.

As the weather worsened, more people who wanted to avoid it came in off the street. The other bellman was much more focused on removing the squatting street people than I was. I learned from my observations when Max was in the back office that the average time in the lobby for the street people was about twenty minutes. By that time, they were warm and ready to go to their next stop, unscheduled as that might be. So unless Max was looking, I took a walk-slow approach to the problem, and it usually solved itself.

My counterpart bellman had a lot of Max in him. When he wasn't running room service, he was consumed with border patrol. He was a Doberman, and they were unwelcome trespassers. There might have been some advantages to his approach since the downtrodden men just had to see him to beat their path for the exit.

While my colleague was working, I was hypnotized by the blowing wind and snow, comfortably killing time in a lobby wing chair. From my perch, I watched the Saturday night crowd streaming into the Algonquin. When my counterpart had some free time, we retired to the kitchen and each had a hotel dessert. It was relaxing and pleasant, secure and warm—almost like home but with more food. I had little hope that Thomas and Danielle would have a soft landing after that night, especially if he maintained the same single-minded gusto he had showed earlier. After we finished our desserts, Granger called, and my bellman colleague was off and running. I told the desk clerk that if Thomas came in to tell him to call home. Then I braved the elements and wandered over to the Algonquin.

Art was packing them in that night, and the crowd was more upscale than his usual clientele. A traveling troupe was playing both a matinee and an evening performance at the municipal auditorium, and this was part of the audience. As I scanned the Algonquin, I saw that Art was not in either of his two usual spots, and I assumed that he would not be making an appearance.

That night the Algonquin was hugely hospitable. The theatre crowd dusted a soft veneer over its usual working-class finish. In the last twenty-four hours, a number of loud, tasteless, but cheery Christmas decorations had came out of boxes and were festooned above the bar and windows. People were in a holiday spirit. The buzz around the room was all about Thanksgiving plans.

Although displaced from the foreground, the pillars of the Algonquin community were still there. Mike and Horace sat behind half-empty beers intently watching the television. Eddie and No-Name were having an animated conversation further down the bar. Eddie seemed well behaved and sober. He was smiling and also seemed pleasantly afflicted by the holiday fever. Most of the other regulars or semi-regulars—and, for better or worse, I now had to consider myself among that number—were also taking an Algonquin refuge from the early snow shower that night. It was genuinely warming to see the many happy exchanges between the newcomers and the seasoned customers.

A familiar couple, well known to me and belonging to neither group, sat in Art's usual corner booth. At first I did not recognize them and I thought they were two of the theatergoers. However, as soon as they saw me and waved me over, I placed them. It was Marco and Sherlene. Marco was wearing a suit and looked sharp. Sherlene was surprisingly stylish in a conservative dress. Her hair was under tight control. They both looked terrific, not in character, but terrific.

As I walked to their booth, they seemed genuinely happy to see me.

"Hey, bellboy," Marco greeted me. "Happy Thanksgiving. Let me buy you a drink." Sherlene smiled broadly.

"Happy Thanksgiving to you," I said. "Are you going to the play?"

"No, no," Marco said, smiling. "We're just having a nice evening out. We're going to dinner later."

"This is the first time I've seen you in here. This is a good crowd tonight."

"Yeah, it's good. We used to come here a lot, before you started working at the hotel." Marco looked at Sherlene and she nodded. "Then one night we ran into some customers and their dates. It was a little, uh … awkward for them. So we thought it might be a good idea not to make it a habit. We only come in here once in a while these days. How 'bout with you?"

"I've been coming here a lot." I said, almost proudly. "Actually, the first time I came here was to get Eileen a sandwich."

"And the rubbers too, right?" interjected Sherlene.

"Yes, rubbers too."

There was a pause while the bar erupted in a cheer for something happening on the television.

"How is Eileen?" I asked, hoping it wasn't a sore subject.

"Oh, I called her and she's real good," said Sherlene like a caring older sister.

Marco had a different take. "She was getting burned out, and when the old lady died, that was pretty much the end of the story for her."

I nodded.

"She's back with her people. That's real good for her," said Sherlene. "She should stay there and never leave again. She'll be a lot happier."

There was a pause again. Then Marco changed the subject.

"We're heading out of here tomorrow," he said.

I was surprised.

"We're going south. This first snow moved up our timetable a little, but we always head down south for the winter."

"Where do you go?"

"Well, it kind of depends on the business climate. We like Tampa, but my contacts down there think the business climate isn't too great right now."

"You mean the police situation?" I said, hoping that it wasn't rude.

"Yes, exactly," said Marco. He seemed to appreciate my grasp of the situation.

He continued. "So this year, we think we're going to go all the way to Miami—Fort Lauderdale, anyway. We like it better there anyway. We'll pull out tomorrow morning if we don't have too much snow tonight. We should make Nashville tomorrow night, then the next night in Jacksonville, and then down the coast to Miami the next day." He looked up and added, "I read in the paper the weather's going to be good the whole way."

"This is kind of like our vacation," said Sherlene, taking his arm.

"Well, I'll tell you something else," said Marco, dropping his voice as if taking me into his confidence. "We may be giving up this line of work. Sherlene wants to give it up and become a waitress. I'll probably get a day job too. We gotta see how things go, but there may be some changes."

"Yeah, it's been getting old for me," said Sherlene. "It's a hard job."

"That's exciting," I said.

"And there's one other thing," said Marco, a little twinkle in his eyes. "We may be getting married soon too." He looked at her lovingly.

Sherlene beamed at him.

"Congratulations," I said.

I noticed Danielle behind us at another table but within earshot even in the noisy bar, and I thought I saw her freeze at the mention of the phrase "getting married."

I congratulated them again, wished them a safe trip, and then excused myself to watch the football game on television.

As I walked through the crowd, Danielle made her way to me.

"Can you come back to the kitchen to talk for a second?" she asked. Without waiting for a response, she led me back to the quieter kitchen.

As the kitchen door swung closed behind us, she turned and spoke.

"I'm supposed to meet Thomas here tonight when my shift is over. But I'm not going to. I'm leaving in a few minutes. I want you to tell him that I left and that I'll talk to him tomorrow." She took on a serious tone.

I hesitated and then said, "I don't think that's a good idea."

"Trust me," she said emphatically. "It's a great idea. I just can't deal with him tonight."

"Should I ask him to call you?" I asked, trying to salvage something for Thomas.

"No. I'll call him tomorrow."

"Will you be at home?"

"Look," she said angrily, "I don't know where I'm going to be. Mom's watching Jenny, and I don't know what I'm doing. He shouldn't come by my place. Just tell him to call me tomorrow and we'll talk." Then she walked away.

I was still back near the kitchen when I saw her slip out the front door a few moments later. I was lost in thought about how I would deliver this information to Thomas. As I shuffled along the crowded bar, deep in thought, I wasn't paying close attention to all the patrons around me. A huge hand reached across my chest and stopped me.

"Hey, how are you?" asked Eddie enthusiastically. His never-to-be named friend had his head in his beer and was focused only on the television.

"I'm fine. How are you tonight?"

"Good, real good. We have a lot of strangers in here tonight, don't we?"

"Yes, the secret's out."

"That's good news and bad news, isn't it? Bad for us, but good for Uncle Art."

I nodded, surprised, since I didn't know that the ownership of the bar was common knowledge.

"I guess it is good for him," I agreed.

"Like he needs any more money," said Eddie.

I played dumb. "Is he pretty wealthy?"

"You can't imagine how much dough he has," Eddie said with great certainty. "I think he owns the college, and he's going to sell it

143

to Purdue." Eddie gave a dumb laugh and then took a large draft of the beer in front of him. "So what are you doing for Thanksgiving? They serve you a big turkey over there at the hotel?"

"No," I said. "I'm going to a friend's house for the holiday."

"Yeah, that'll be good. I'm probably going to go out to a restaurant if my cousin doesn't give me a call. It'll be good to take the time off, though, won't it?"

"Yes, I'm looking forward to it," I said.

Eddie then turned back to his beer, his friend, and the television.

"Hey, I'll see you around," he said, and he did not wait for an answer.

Danielle was to have covered the shift until ten, and from nine o'clock on, I posted myself near the door to intercept Thomas. The suit-coat crowd had thinned by then and we were back to the regulars. I don't think Mike or Horace moved in the time I was there. The other regulars were also engrossed in the television. Eddie and his friend were now drinking shots and beers.

At a little before ten, Thomas walked in. I tried to usher him out so we could talk privately, but he hesitated, looking for Danielle. I finally managed to pull him out to the sidewalk to have the talk.

The snow had stopped and the wind was less intense. The streets were messy with about an inch of slush on the sidewalk.

"Okay, what?" he said to me.

"It's about Danielle ..."

"What? What's wrong?"

"Nothing's wrong. She just told me to tell you that she was leaving early."

"Why, is there something wrong with Jenny?"

"I don't think so. I think she just wanted to leave early."

"Well, all right. I'll go over and see what's going on," he said as he started to walk away.

"Thomas, wait. She said her mother was watching Jenny, and she told me to tell you not to come over. She'll call you tomorrow."

"Is she at her apartment or at her mother's house?"

"I have no idea. But she gave me the impression that she wanted to be alone tonight."

"Why?"

"I don't know."

At that moment, Eddie and his friend came out of the bar.

"Hey," said Eddie. "It's my little friend the piano player." His tone was irritating though not hostile.

"We're talking here," said Thomas.

"What are you talking about? Music or the great quitters of the sports world?"

"Get lost," said Thomas.

Eddie was less playful now.

"Lost? Hey, All-Star, I've been lost for a while," he said, coming in very close to Thomas's face.

"I just want to say one thing," he said.

Eddie hooked his leg under Thomas's legs, and Thomas went down in the slush in a heap.

Eddie gave a cruel laugh.

"I just wanted to tell you not to slip in the snow."

Thomas jumped quickly to his feet and pushed Eddie hard in the chest. Eddie moved back a little but not much.

Eddie then gave Thomas a push. Thomas went backward and nearly fell, but he came back swinging this time.

Eddie saw the first punch and moved to the side. The blow hit him on the shoulder and caused no harm.

Eddie squared his arms. Thomas had his fists ready to deliver another punch. Eddie was sizing him up when the toot of a police siren rang out from the street. A voice over a bullhorn stopped them.

The policeman in his cruiser told them to break it up or they would both land in jail.

They hesitated, still eying one another warily. The policeman told them again to break it up. Eddie pulled his hands down and walked away with his friend. Thomas stood there with me watching him go.

After Eddie turned the block, Thomas looked at me.

"I'm going to find Danielle. I'll see you later."

CHAPTER 18

I looked forward to being back at work and avoiding any further involvement in their situation. The role of a relationship counselor did not play to my strengths. Even a 101 class in relationship management would be too advanced for me, and I was being immersed in a high-level graduate class with those two. I wouldn't do well, and more to the point, I wasn't skillful enough to be of much service to Thomas and Danielle. I had no interest in participating in the drama. I wanted to hide from both of them.

As it turned out, I was working the next night, Sunday. I was taking off the Thanksgiving Thursday, and my cooperative usual weekend relief bellman was fine with swapping Sunday for Thanksgiving. The hotel, it seems, provided a wonderful Thanksgiving dinner for the staff who were required to work. The usual Sunday dinner was canceled because of the holiday offering. Dinner that Sunday for me was a sausage link sandwich and on Thursday for him it was turkey and trimmings. Still, it was good to be working.

Work was slow. Granger apparently was well provisioned from the evening before, judging from how quiet he was. The other guests were generally content and either did not need my services or had left town early for the holiday. There were very few patrons in the hotel.

The snow from last night vanished with the afternoon sunlight, but the temperature dropped again at sunset. There were no homeless drop-in's thus far, to my relief. I assumed that they were not on the move on Sundays. After my modest dinner, I sat in the lobby gazing vacantly out the window. The Algonquin looked quiet. I watched the evening traffic pass while daydreaming about what I might do in the spring. I did not have a job lined up but felt excited about going back home or at least about leaving school. As I tried losing myself in these future musings, I noticed Danielle and Thomas suddenly appear on the Algonquin doorstep. I didn't know if they were coming or going.

They were arguing. Under the street lamp, they carried on for several minutes, until Danielle appeared to break into tears and abruptly walked away. Thomas ran after her and looked apologetic when he caught her. She stopped and listened. Their interchange was less heated than the one moments before. As they started back toward the Algonquin, he reached down to hold her hand. They walked past the restaurant and disappeared around the corner.

It was about ten o'clock when I saw them leave. There were no other activities going on, and I took full advantage of the lull to start my evening chores of vacuuming, cleaning ashtrays, and emptying any lobby trash. I was making good progress, hoping my early evening industry would pay off with several hours of uninterrupted sleep later in the night.

Just before midnight, I was surprised to see Eddie stroll in to the lobby. I was in the corner working, and although I saw him, I didn't speak up. He looked around until he saw me and walked up to me.

He asked me in a quiet voice, "Have you seen Danielle?"

I was surprised by the question.

He sounded concerned, like an older brother. He did not seem drunk at all.

"She hasn't been in here tonight," I answered truthfully. "Actually, I've never seen her in here."

"Is Thomas here?" he continued.

"No. He doesn't work at night, and I haven't seen him in here tonight either."

He thought for a moment, thanked me politely, and walked out. I didn't ask him if he wanted to leave either of them a message.

I continued my housekeeping duties until the lobby was in acceptable condition for the next day. The desk remained quiet. The mail, newspapers, and pastries would not be calling me for another several hours. I told the night clerk that I was done and asked him if he had any problem with me going up to the mezzanine for a nap. I was rarely able to do this, but there was a long sofa there within earshot of the desk if he called me. It sounded far more inviting than one of the lobby chairs. With his approval, I climbed the lobby stairs and looked forward to a long nap.

I had wonderful expectations for those next five hours. They would represent a new personal record for me at the Lafayette. On the couch, I fell asleep immediately. I was in a deep sleep when I stirred to the voices and then awoke to the shouts. It was a man and a woman making the noise. A woman was doing the shouting. I checked my watch and saw that it was after three.

Thomas and Danielle were sitting in a corner of the lobby, and were it not for the volume of their argument, they might have been reasonably inconspicuous.

"You just don't understand, Thomas," she screamed. "I don't want this anymore."

"Please, please" was his only response. "Danielle, please."

"We have totally different goals. I don't want what you want. I don't want to be where you want to be. I don't want the life you want."

"I can change," he pleaded.

"Thomas, no you can't!"

"Yes, I can. Danielle, I love you. I'll do anything for you."

"No. It's not going to work, and I don't want it to work," she screamed again. "I don't love you. I've never loved you the way you love me, Thomas. It's not enough. I'm sorry. Good-bye."

She stood to leave, and he stood to hold her.

She pushed him off and said, "Leave me alone. Don't try to see me or Jenny ever again."

Then she walked off again and he stayed. He stood for a little, while unsure of what to do. Then he sat quietly in the chair. The silence of the hotel was haunting. Thomas buried his head in his hands. In a few moments, the quiet gave way to the sound of his sobs filling the empty room.

It was painful as I listened to him cry for what seemed an eternity. Eventually, I descended the stairs and sat next to him. He cried for some time more while I sat with him, and neither of us uttered a word.

Finally, he just looked up at me. All he said was "Thanks."

Then he walked to the piano and played. It was sad and dramatic and all classical music. I sat next to him on the piano bench the entire time; he seemed to enjoy the comfort of my unvoiced support.

At almost five, he stopped his play. He looked at me and said, "Thanks again." Then he walked outside to the new day.

The rest of the week would pass without further drama. Later that morning, I did not see Thomas at work. On Tuesday I again waited for him to start his shift, but he didn't show up. I went to the Algonquin before my shift and learned that Danielle had called in sick that day. Ben and Art were off to spend the Thanksgiving holiday with their respective grandchildren. Ernie and Pete decided to travel together, heading somewhere south for the long weekend. There was little atmosphere in the place.

On Wednesday morning I waited again for Thomas. This time Hal saw me and asked me what I knew about Thomas. He had not been to work that week and had not called in his absences. Hal had telephoned his apartment; no one answered the phone. Hal, usually Thomas's greatest fan, was not pleased. He had to pay a plumber for a job he knew Thomas could have done. He threatened to take the plumber's payment out of Thomas's next paycheck. He asked me to pass the threat on to Thomas, which implied some conspiracy of silence on my part about Thomas's whereabouts.

After classes, about three in the afternoon, I stopped by both the Algonquin and the hotel to look for the quarreling parties. Neither of them had been seen at either place. While at the hotel I received a call from Margery, who wanted to know if I had seen Thomas.

"Has something happened?" she asked.

I didn't know if I should share what I had witnessed. I sighed. I couldn't lie to her. "Danielle broke up with him."

There was silence on the other end for a moment. Then she said, "Oh, no. I thought their relationship was going well. How do you think Thomas is doing?"

"I don't know."

There was fear in her voice when she said, "Julian, please stop by his apartment and tell him to come home."

"I will."

After the call, I drove to Thomas's apartment. I did not see his car but knew that since he did not live too far from the hotel, he often left it there. I hadn't checked the lot before I drove to see him. His apartment lights were off in the darkening late afternoon, but the other units were similarly dark. I went to the door and listened, but there was no sound inside. I knocked on the door and waited; then I knocked again. There was no answer. I went down to the mail drop on the first floor and picked up a piece of junk mail. I ripped off a piece of an envelope and scrawled a note that I stuck in the doorjamb. When I returned to the hotel for my shift that night, I called Thomas again and received no answer. I also called Margery. She was confident that no matter what else was going on Thomas would be at the farm on Thanksgiving Day.

I called Thomas a few more times during the night. There was still no answer. After my shift, Hal was waiting for me to see if I had any idea where Thomas might be. Hal was on the warpath and wanted to scream at someone. His required appearance on Thanksgiving morning did not improve his mood. He had another problem with the hotel plumbing and didn't want to pay retail when he had Thomas on the payroll. Hal was not happy, and when I couldn't help him, he turned his anger at me. Having only another few weeks there anyway, I just turned and walked away from him. I drove back to Thomas's apartment, thinking he might be preparing to come to the farm. I was hoping to catch him before he left. I didn't want to have to repeat Hal's threats to him in Margery's presence. His car was not in the hotel lot. I saw it parked in front of his building on the street when I drove up. There were no lights on, but my note had been removed. There was no mail left for his place on the first floor. If he had had mail, he had retrieved it.

I knocked. No response. I knocked again; still no response. I had a sense that he was in there, and I spoke to the closed door. If he wouldn't open the door, I begged him to at least call his mother about the day. I left him another note after I tired of talking to the closed door. I indicated that he had some challenging conversations ahead of him at the Lafayette if he expected to keep his job there. Then I told him or the door that I hoped I would see him later at the farm and left.

CHAPTER 19

I thought about the end of college as I drove to the farm. It would be over in two weeks. Despite a near-death accident, ridiculous debt, and my mother's death, I had managed to finish. Now what? I had applied to journalism school, and I was waiting for admissions and the financial-aid process to proceed before I could make any decisions. The war continued, and I was passed over but not untouched. No one my age did not have friends who were drafted and in combat. I stood on the sidelines while they were in the game. Before there was the guilt of survivorship, there was the guilt of evasion. Our privilege was to pursue our dreams and ideals, but we were dependent on them to live out our heroism and patriotism. I was never comfortable with that dependency.

I wondered where Thomas stood in the draft. I did feel sad for him, and I hoped that he would not lay his hands on a pistol again. Then I put the terrible thought out of my mind. Although girlfriends had dumped me before, I had never been dumped by one who was carrying my child. I couldn't imagine how that felt. Thomas had to move on with his life. He had to leave town and find a new start. He wasn't doing much for himself there. I imagined Margery would tell me as much later that afternoon.

Turning off the paved road and up the farm's long gravel driveway, I strained to see if Thomas's car was there. I did not see it but still hoped he had parked in the barn. It was cold, so I was not surprised that Margery did not come out to greet me. I parked in front of the house, and she opened the door with a big smile when I came up the steps. If she was disappointed that Thomas was not with me, she did not show it.

I said hello to her, and she gave me a dignified hug and ushered me in. I looked around, and she immediately picked up on what I was thinking.

"I haven't heard from him yet," she said. Her tone was flat and neither sad nor angry. "I'm sure he'll be along before supper. Come on in and tell me how you are doing."

The room was warm with the sounds of a crackling wood fire and the smells of a great meal cooking. We talked for nearly an hour.

"What will you be doing when you graduate, Julian?"

"Margery, believe it or not, I'm only just coming to grips with that. I've applied to graduate school in journalism, but I don't know how that will work out. I have no savings, no steady girlfriend, and no immediate prospects for a job other than as a night bellman."

"Maybe you'll stay on at the hotel and keep an eye on Thomas for me?"

"I don't think so, Margery," I said apologetically. "I've got to make a move."

"I know you do, Julian. But I thought I'd ask."

I nodded and then said, "Tell me how you're getting along these days with Thomas out of town. How are you keeping busy?"

She talked about how she was still active at the church and in town, volunteering at the senior center. We talked about how the crops went with her renters last season. We talked about the farm generally, and she discussed her concerns about the more expensive maintenance the farm would need in the future. Except for highlighting how Thomas would contribute to the maintenance effort, she did not mention him at all.

Glancing at a mantle clock she then broke off the conversation, announcing that she had work to do in the kitchen. Dinner would be in an hour. She was clear that my help was unneeded and steered me outside to take a walk and build up my appetite. Since there was no refusing her, I put on my hat, gloves, and coat and went outdoors like a child being sent out to play.

The farm was stark in its solitude and prewinter austerity. The frozen ground was easy for walking even with the coating of snow. Without the wind, it might have been almost comfortable, but as it was, gusting snow pelted my glasses and forced me to stop often to clean them. Since I was just walking to kill time, I went downwind first, gambling that the near gale would lessen or shift direction by the time I returned.

I felt strange being on the farm and making this walk without Thomas. I had only been on this ground once in the truck, and I did not feel that my first hike here should be done without him. As the wind directed me, I took the trail to the pond and the orchard, Thomas's orchard. I tried to remember which of the trees had been granted a name, but I could not distinguish them. They all looked the same, and I saw the phantoms of his boyhood as the branches seemed to reach for me in the wind. As I left the orchard, I had to resist the urge to look over my shoulder, afraid that one of the trees would, indeed, move to seize me.

After the orchard, the land fell away and displayed the pond below. There were ducks on the pond, but it had begun to ice around the margins. The ducks barely looked at me as I walked by. They tucked their heads into their wings and bore down against the wind. I took my leave from them. I had had enough. The wind was freshening, and I turned back into it before it blew even harder.

I walked back briskly and double-timed my walk through the orchard. I still had some time left before dinner, and sensing that Margery wanted the time to prepare, I slipped into the barn. In the dying light, I found the ladder to the loft and ascended to the spot that Thomas had showed me on our last trip. The wind howled through the open hay door in the loft. I didn't stay long, but I did linger long enough to drink in Thomas's favorite view and to remember his disappointment that his sister never saw it.

The naked trees were silent sentries around the plowed fields. Ducks on the wing coming to the pond were silhouetted in the slate sky with the blowing snow. It was austere but peaceful. It was a peace that Thomas talked about but never seemed to find.

I descended the ladder quickly and hastened my steps back to the house. For some reason, I expected Thomas to have arrived. Bounding up the back porch steps, I saw Margery, now in a pretty dress. I had hoped to see Thomas by her side, but he was not there.

"How was your walk?" she asked casually as I entered the kitchen.

"Brisk," I said, removing my gloves. "Has Thomas come yet?"

She smiled weakly and shook her head.

"Supper's ready in five minutes. It's all set, and there's nothing for you to do except open a bottle of wine if you want it."

She paused, watching my expression. Then she added, "If you feel guilty, you can do most of the cleanup."

I washed my hands, opened the bottle, and poured my glass. She did not drink. I felt underdressed, as she was in her Sunday finest with pearls and high heels. She brought the bird to the table fully carved. She was not expecting only one guest, but she did not let on that it bothered her or that she was disappointed.

Thomas's absence or the reason for it was the elephant in the room, and after my first serving, during my settling period, I brought up the subject.

"Margery, I'm so sorry for you that Thomas didn't come."

She looked at me and nodded. "I am too."

"I think that the relationship he's been in has really been consuming him," I said, feeling that I had to make an excuse. "But I think he'll be all right," I continued without any basis for my conclusion.

"I'm not worried, if that's what you are trying to say." She paused and then continued. "I almost lost him two years ago, and the Lord pulled him back to me. It's up to God now. He's in charge."

She paused again.

"So don't you worry either." She smiled, lightening her mood. "Have some more mashed potatoes."

I did, and we did not mention Thomas for the rest of the meal. Instead we spoke of music and the piano. Or rather she talked, and I ate, listened, and learned. It was thoroughly delightful.

After dinner, as we agreed, I cleaned up by myself. Margery played the piano while I washed the dishes. I wanted Thomas to burst through the front door for her sake, but my hopes died with the daylight.

Afterward, I poured another glass of wine, put a log on the fire, and relaxed to her playing. The teacher in her was compelled to announce the title and the composer before she played. She even told a little about the life of the composer and where the music was composed. It was mostly Chopin and Mozart, although she spiced it with Gershwin and, in the holiday spirit, Irving Berlin. It was a recital worth good money.

When she tired of playing she came over and sat across from me.

"How did you meet Thomas's father?" I asked.

The piano playing had put her in a nostalgic mood, and she seemed to want to share.

"James and I both grew up in Gary. He was two years older, but I'd had a crush on him since I was ten years old. Times were tough then. It was the Depression, and Europe and Asia seemed ready for war. My family was poor, and they really had nothing but their music. They always loved their music." Then she laughed. "My parents would buy me piano lessons almost before they would buy me shoes. It was that important to them."

Then her mood became more serious. "Well, when I was sixteen, it turned into a real shooting war in Europe. James and I had our first date that year. He took me to the movies, and all I remember from that date is how James talked about the newsreel. James was proud and patriotic. He wanted to serve when the war found us too. He joined in '42, right after college. He wanted to fly. He learned to fly in Alabama and, well, I followed him down. We married in '43 just before he went overseas, Europe." She paused thoughtfully. "Those were hard days.

"He made it back sixteen months later. It was difficult getting to know him again, to tell the truth. He was changed in many ways. He was so hard, so proud, and so closed. I had moved back home, and he took a posting as a training officer up here in Indiana so we could be closer. Well, some stupid things went on down on the base about getting into the officer's club. There was a fight, and it was ugly. Suddenly, James didn't want the military anymore. He felt disrespected. He left the service as soon as he could. He found that he loved engineering. Thomas was born while James was in graduate school."

"Thomas must have marked a real turning point in your life, especially with the end of the war," I said.

That's right," she said. "Life started to ease up a little after Thomas was born. James was out of school and had a good job. We were able to buy this farm on his salary—land was a lot cheaper back then. Life was very good."

She took a sip of her coffee. "Then we had Jeanie, and we knew she was sick right away. She had a heart problem. We went to all kinds of specialists, but they couldn't help her. When she was six, she caught a cold that led to pneumonia. Her heart wasn't strong enough to keep up with the infection. She died upstairs while James and I held her hands. Thomas cried for a week."

She paused, having difficulty with speaking, and looked at me earnestly. "When you're a parent, there's nothing in this world that hurts like the death of your child."

Neither of us spoke for a few minutes. Then she started again.

"Thomas became a different boy after Jeanie's death. James and I were focused on trying to help each other get over it. You never do, of course, but even just getting beyond it is so hard. While we were looking after one another, Thomas was looking after himself. He became independent, but in a good way. He never bothered us. He excelled at all the things that mattered to him. Maybe he thought that we would pay more attention to him if he did."

I didn't say anything as she continued.

"Thomas did fine until James died, but James's death crushed him. It came as a complete shock to Thomas, although I knew James was smoking too much and not taking care of himself. He had been having chest pains but ignored them and didn't see a doctor. He said he was feeling fine, and then one night he just passed in his sleep. That's when all the nervous issues started with Thomas." She gazed out the window as if looking for him to come in.

"He's a good boy. He's a good son."

"I can see that," I said. "I really think he lives for you and this farm."

She finished her coffee and walked the cup to the kitchen. She stopped there and cleaned a spot I missed off the countertop.

She returned and smiled at me. "I'm going to bed now. Thank you, Julian, for spending Thanksgiving with me. It would have been lonelier without you. Why don't you stay down here and finish that bottle of wine. Otherwise it will go to waste."

I thanked her again for the day as she climbed the stairs. I poured the last of the bottle and reviewed the day, not at all sure that Thomas was going to be fine.

I went to bed around eleven, having been quickly caught up in a book I brought with me. At midnight, the telephone rang. On the second ring, Margery picked it up in her room and I could only hear some muffled sounds as she spoke to the caller in her calm voice.

Coming to breakfast the next morning, I was again delighted by the smells of the kitchen. Coffee and the newspaper were waiting for me. Margery made small talk about the weather and did not refer to the telephone call. If she was not going to mention it, neither was I.

After the breakfast cleanup, I asked her if there were any chores that needed doing while I was there. She refused any of my help. It was late morning, so I prepared to leave. I was working that night and had some class work to attend to before I went to the hotel. As I left, she handed me a satchel containing cold weather clothes for Thomas. I happily agreed to deliver it and then went on my way after she gave me a hug and an open invitation to return any time I wanted.

When I reached town, I immediately drove to Thomas's apartment. The lights were off and his car was not there. There was no answer to my knocks on the door. I left the clothes on his threshold and hoped that he would find them.

CHAPTER 20

I turned the calendar page to December and really felt like a "short-timer." The first week of December passed quickly, as I had to shore up some neglected academic responsibilities. I had yet to see Thomas. However, I did know that someone was turning on his lights and moving his car. He would not answer his door, although the clothes had been picked up. I did not see him, and he did not return to work.

Hal fired him from the Lafayette, or he would have if Thomas had bothered to make an appearance. For a week after Thanksgiving, Hal came to work early each day just to ask me if I had seen him. He would usually interrupt my breakfast, and since I had grown to cherish my routine, I found Hal's presence extremely irritating. Whether he sensed my mood or just grew tired of asking I wasn't sure, but at least he stopped asking and I could enjoy my morning coffee alone again.

I was looking forward to the break after the semester. I still didn't have a good sense of the magnitude of the break, but I knew that I would have some time to myself; how much time was still partially a matter for the fates to determine.

The weather had turned simply miserable for so early in the season. We had had snow and cold, but now the cold was hovering in the teens and had dipped to single digits at night. My predawn mail run was becoming increasingly hazardous to my health. Snow covered the ground, and the salt was having little effect on the ice. The river already had ice crusting over the shallows. Even worse, this frigid December introduction came after a particularly cold November, and people were already tiring of a winter that had not yet officially started.

I hadn't seen Art and the other old men together in weeks. I stopped by the Algonquin on Saturday afternoon. Art was in his usual corner booth with coffee and a newspaper. He seemed genuinely glad to see me when I walked in.

"Hello, Art," I said. "How was your Thanksgiving?"

"Just fine. How about yours?"

"Very enjoyable," I said. I did not want to go into the fact that I had been to Thomas's farm, remembering that Art was Thomas's ultimate employer. "Where are the three professors?" I asked.

Art explained that Ernie was still on his Thanksgiving holiday trip. Ben was off with family, and neither he nor Ernie would be back until after the New Year. Peter was expected in later in the day.

"I'm sorry I missed them. Next week is my last week."

"I remember," said Art. "It all went by pretty quick, didn't it?"

"Yes, but I've enjoyed working here," I said.

"I wasn't talking about the job. I was talking about your college years."

"Yes, those too."

He took a sip of his coffee. "Do you know what you're going to do?"

I told him I didn't but that I had some applications in for graduate school and that I wasn't in any danger of being drafted.

"You'll do fine. If you have any problems, come back here and I'll take care of you."

"Thanks, Art. I appreciate that." I felt sincerely flattered by the offer.

He took another drink of his coffee and changed the subject. "I heard your friend Thomas is missing in action."

"Yes, I haven't seen him since before Thanksgiving."

"Any idea what happened to him?"

"No."

"Well, I guess you know he and Danielle were dating," Art said.

I nodded, and he continued. "She's missing too."

"Really?" I didn't see those two running off together after the fight I saw.

"Yes. I called her house. Her mother answered the phone and told me that Danielle was leaving for a few weeks. Her mom was watching Jenny, but she didn't say anything about Thomas."

"I hadn't heard anything about that," I said.

"I told her mother to have her give me a call. I don't mind losing Thomas—a kid that talented was never going to stay as a hotel handyman. But I don't like losing Danielle. She's the spirit of this place."

"I see your point."

"If Thomas has left, I suppose I have one less worry about this place, though."

"I don't follow you," I said.

"It's one less thing my nephew can screw up. It turns down some of the heat for a bar fight here."

"I still don't follow you."

"You know—Eddie. He's my nephew. He's my youngest sister's kid, and he's always been a little crazy. He's not a bad person, but he is a miserable drunk. I was always worried that Eddie and Thomas were going to start something in here that would break up the place.

I was thinking I would have to throw one of them out, but Thomas seems to have made it easy for me."

"Yeah, I guess so," I said absently.

"I know it was hard on him with Thomas and Danielle," Art continued. "But I'm glad nothing got out of hand."

"Why was it so hard on him? Danielle didn't give Eddie a lot of attention."

Art smiled at me.

"You don't know the history here. Eddie is the father of Danielle's little girl."

It took me a few moments to process what I had just heard. "I didn't know that," I muttered.

"Oh, yes," he said. "Eddie and Danielle dated for years, even after she had the baby and refused to marry him. Eddie is helping to raise that little girl financially—well actually, I've been helping her, and I make sure Eddie gives her the money I give him before he drinks it away. I think Eddie tries to be as big a part of her life as Danielle lets him, which isn't too much these days. Even though Eddie and Danielle squabble, I think they have, you know, 'an understanding,' and it's more than just because of Jenny. They just know each other so well they don't carry on too much when other people are around."

For a moment, I was speechless. Then I asked, "Does Thomas know?"

Art thought for a moment.

"I assumed he does, but I'm not really sure. I can't imagine that she hid it from him."

I stayed indoors the rest of the weekend and hoped that my furnace would not surrender. It was a losing battle in my drafty apartment, but as long as the temperature stayed above sixty, I was counting my blessings. The next week flew by. I drove past Thomas's place a few times. Sometimes the lights were on and sometimes they were off. I stopped several times, but lights or not, there was no answer at his door. I hoped he had called Margery. I called her a few times intending to tell her that Thomas seemed to be at home, but I was happy not to have reached her. I didn't want to hear the disappointment in her voice. Either she had spoken with him or took it on her great faith that he was healthy.

My last day at the Lafayette came without my seeing him. It was the last day of the last pay period I would enjoy at the hotel. I ran my last mail delivery, sorted my last papers, and pinched my last donuts. I officially retired my red bellman's vest. The payroll clerk agreed to have my check ready the next day.

I returned to my cold apartment for a cool shower and a few hours of sleep before returning to the hotel that afternoon. After collecting my paycheck, I went to Hal's office and made my good-byes there.

He was sitting at his desk.

"This is it, then?" he said as I came through his door.

"Yes, Hal. This is it," I said with a smile and shook his extended hand.

"You promise me that when you get to Vietnam, you'll send me a letter and a picture of you in uniform?"

"I promise," I said.

"This night bellman experience has been a good one for you. You're a good worker. After a couple of years in the army, you'll be able to make something of yourself. It might even fix what those college professors did to your brain."

"I'm sure you're right, Hal."

"Take care of yourself, kid. It's been a pleasure having you work here."

"Thanks, Hal. I've enjoyed it." It occurred to me that I really had.

I had already said my farewell to Max. I went to see Granger and hoped it would be brief. It was. He shook my hand and, with his stubby, yellow-stained fingers, managed to pull a five-dollar bill out of his wallet. He handed it to me and told me earnestly that I deserved every nickel of the tip for the great service I had given him the last four months. I thanked him and considered that great praise.

I lingered in the lobby for a few minutes after seeing Granger. There were few Christmas decorations around; just a little plastic garland over the lobby desk. The wing chairs stood in their usual places. They had not been moved since Thomas's last concert. The piano key cover was starting to collect dust, although the housekeeping staff kept the soundboard lid well polished. No one else was in the lobby, and no one else was coming. It was quiet like a tomb, and it was almost Christmas.

CHAPTER 21

After collecting my final paycheck and my last piece of advice from Hal, I was in festive mood. My classes and exams were finished. I was a now a graduate, or would be when one final paper was submitted and my grades were issued. I thought of my own family and a promise kept. I thought of having endured the rehab after my accident and of escaping with only one bad eye as a residual. It was Christmastime, and I had no obligations and a little bit of cash in my pocket. I would be leaving for home in the morning.

While I made my final rounds at the Lafayette, the weather had turned from merely miserable to truly abominable. The afternoon snow that earlier drifted gently down on the hotel entrance was now wind driven, horizontal, and twice as heavy as just a few hours earlier. The temperature had worsened with the wind, and the snow was accumulating rapidly. But to be honest, except for its potential to delay my morning departure, I really didn't care. It could not have dampened my mood. The harder it snowed, the happier I became, because I had no obligations. I was free. I could walk to my apartment and leave my car in the hotel lot if the roads became much worse. I was on no one's schedule but my own.

I walked across the street to take a long last look down the town's main street. I wanted to soak it in, since I knew I wouldn't be coming back here for a long time. I stared at the bridge over the heavy brown water and the snow covering the ice except in the fastest center channel. It was a leap of memory to think of the children with their cane poles on the embankment just months earlier. I would likely never see that sight again here. That chapter of my life was now over, but I took joy in a new beginning.

Tired of the blizzard, no matter how giddy I felt, I decided to adjourn to the Algonquin for my final appearance. It was almost happy hour after all, and I was certainly feeling happy.

The Algonquin looked more festive than I remembered it from just days before. I noticed the tinsel around the top-shelf bottles. I noticed the Santa cutout over the cash register. Plastic pine garlands and twinkle lights were strung down one side of the bar and up the other. Both the bartender and the waitresses wore Santa hats. It felt like Christmas.

Art was in his booth, and it looked like he had a drink in front of him rather than coffee, which was unusual. I took that as a good sign. The place was altogether fitting for my mood.

As unpleasant as the weather was outside, the patrons and employees were working together to make it festive, welcoming, and hospitable inside. Mike and Horace were smiling and chatting up the barman. The television was off; instead, music—Christmas carols—was playing over the radio. No one complained.

I was a celebrity of sorts that night in the bar. Over the past months, the regulars had embraced me as one of their own, and word escaped that I would be departing their fond bosom. "Forever" gone sounded too harsh, especially with every good citizens of the Algonquin buying me a drink. But that was how it was going to be. All of these generous people would die to me after that night. That was life. That's what happened. That was graduation day.

Judging by the people coming in, many of the local businesses must have released staff early because of the storm. New customers popped in off the street, shivering and snow covered; they shook themselves off and joined the others. They were all strangers to me, but we were all happy strangers with one another. Even they wanted to buy me a drink when they heard my story of imminent departure.

My benefactors included Eddie and No-Name. They were among the snowiest arrivals, suggesting that they had been out the longest. It was immediately obvious that their pedestrian journey had originated at another bar and that the Algonquin was certainly not their first stop. They came in with much more fanfare and volume than the others. The nameless friend was louder than Eddie, but both could be heard clearly above the growing din of the Algonquin. It didn't matter. It felt like a magical night. It was just great.

I saw him enter out of the corner of my eye, but I did not recognize him at first. Thomas had joined the throng but was initially screened from my sight by two other men as he entered. He scanned the room, looking alert and agitated, and then disappeared behind a group.

He came my way, although I don't think he saw me. I was in no way angry at him, just relieved and happy that he looked well and was finally out of his apartment. Eddie, now sitting further down the bar, also saw Thomas arrive.

I made my way over to him as he slowly pushed through the crowd. I tapped him on the back, and he turned.

"Hey, are you okay?" I asked with an enthusiasm that was fed by his absence and a few beers. I put my arm around his shoulder. "I missed you."

His gaze continued to dart around the room, and he never made eye contact with me.

"I'm fine." He turned his head from side to side, still searching. "Where's Danielle? Have you seen her?"

"Uh, well ..." I was deciding how much I wanted to share with him there.

With that, Eddie appeared next to us. His enormous frame blocked out the glow of the twinkle lights.

"Danielle hit the road, All-Star. She's gone. Forget about her."

Thomas just glared at him, saying nothing, trying to process.

"She's ancient history to you. Get over it," Eddie continued. He seemed to be enjoying this.

Thomas started to say something when Eddie interrupted.

"You might know that she has this little problem that she was going to take care of while she was gone. She wants nothing to do with you; I mean nothing!" Eddie sneered at Thomas. "How does that sound, All-Star? Do you understand what I'm saying?" Eddie was almost shouting, and most of the patrons stopped to listen.

Thomas had a faraway look. He seemed to be looking well beyond Eddie. "No," he muttered quietly, as if in a trance, almost to himself. "No."

"Oh, yeah," continued Eddie. "She said she's never coming back." The other customers were hanging on every word, and Eddie seemed to enjoy the wider humiliation.

"No!" Thomas said more loudly. The whole bar was watching them, and they heard the sorrow in his voice.

Eddie smiled wickedly.

Thomas seemed to be further detached the more Eddie went on.

"Oh, and one other thing, All-Star. I'm not so sure it was yours." He paused for effect and then continued slowly. "Danielle and I, you know, for old time's sake and all that? Maybe it's me who should be upset."

"No!" he shrieked. It was painful to hear, painful to hear the father of a dying child. All eyes were on them.

Thomas was now in the moment. He was seething.

"So that's the news. Deal with it and get out of my way," said Eddie, sweeping at Thomas with his forearm. The blow caught him by surprise and pushed him into other customers around the bar.

Then the switch went off. Lightning fast, Thomas stepped forward and hit Eddie with a combination jab and cross. He hit him square in the nose, and Eddie was stunned but recovered quickly. Eddie swung wildly with a punch that Thomas saw coming and ducked.

Both were ready to relaunch when Art suddenly appeared from the crowd and stood between them.

His presence there froze both of them. Neither wanted to challenge him. Art waited a few moments, glaring at both of them before he spoke. When he raised his voice to speak, the bar was silent except for the Christmas carol in the background.

"Both of you. Get out of here, now," bellowed Art in an unarguable voice. "If you two can't come into this place without a chip on your shoulder, don't ever come back. Do you understand me?" He stared at each of them, and they both nodded. "Now leave."

The two made their way to the door, and the crowd parted for them. I trailed behind, hoping to speak to Thomas. Eddie rubbed his nose as he walked away. I was close enough to hear him say to Thomas as they passed through the door, "This isn't finished, peanut."

At that moment, I heard Art call me. I turned.

"Look," he said to me firmly, "you don't want to get too involved in this. Let them work it out. Whatever is going to happen is going to happen. Stay out of it. Maybe something good will come of it."

I didn't share Art's optimism. "I hope you're right," I said, "but I have to speak with Thomas."

It took me a few minutes to find my coat in the overfilled coat rack. After buttoning up, I quietly slipped out of the bar. Eddie's friend had found another soul mate and was oblivious to it all. The rest of the crowd partied on as if nothing had happened. The Christmas carols played on.

Once on the street, I started to rethink my strategy. The wind was even stronger and the snow heavier than before. Several more inches had already accumulated on the sidewalk. It was a whiteout, and if I had had great eyes, I would have been challenged. With my glasses, it was hopeless. I looked up and down the sidewalks and saw nothing. I thought of going to the Lafayette, but under the circumstances I didn't think it was likely that I would find him there.

I walked down the block, looked across the bridge, and thought I saw a pedestrian, possibly two, on the far side. Before I was sure, two snowplows slowly passed in front of me, blocking my vision. After the trucks passed, the bridge was deserted.

I wiped my glasses again and crossed the street to the bridge. At about midspan, I caught sight of them down on the path of the river walk. They were fighting. The wind was gusting, howling, and I could hear nothing. I continued across the span and made the turn from the sidewalk down the stairs to the footpath. I rushed down the stairs. The howling wind was louder as it swirled around the stairwell. I slipped and fell down the last five or six stairs and lost my glasses. It took me a minute or so to recover from the fall and to find them.

Rising to my feet, I ran to the path. The snow cut into my face and blurred my vision. I saw no one. I slowed my pace, huddling against the storm until I reached where I thought they had been. The other-world purity of the snow sheet was heavily disturbed there. For a moment the wind died and I could see again. What I saw in the snow I have been unable to forget for forty years. It still comes back to me in dreams.

I had seen it before, just once. It was Eddie's knife. The blade was bloody, and there was blood in the snow all around. Time stopped, and then it comes back to me now as if in slow motion. I don't know how long I stared at the knife before moving.

I looked around again at the drifting snow. Drops and streaks of blood were in the trampled area, and a single set of footprints led away. Then the wind started again and I was blind.

I looked down the embankment. The ice below may have been broken, but I could barely see my hand in front of my face. I could not be sure.

I still can't quite understand my motivation for what happened next. I stared again at the knife. Then I picked it out of the snow and held it in my hand, studying the blood on the blade. Then I threw the knife as far as I could into the center of the river. I knew that whatever happened was over and would not happen again.

I stood there for several minutes watching the snow wipe clean the tracks and purify the bloody ground. I tried to follow the footprints that led away from the Lafayette and the Algonquin and from the last several months. When the prints led to a hard-packed sidewalk, I saw an occasional drop of blood, but then both the footprints and the blood trail vanished.

Following the tracks, I was already halfway back to my apartment. I was cold and confused. I finished the trip home and pondered my next move.

About an hour later, I had thought it all through. I called the Algonquin to speak with Art. I asked him if he had heard anything more from Eddie or Thomas. He hadn't, although he wasn't expecting to since he had thrown them out earlier. He asked me if I had seen any more of them. I told him no; by the time I left the Algonquin they were gone and I couldn't follow them in the storm. I couldn't see anything in the blowing wind even if I wanted to follow them. Art commended me on my good judgment and told me he would get word to me if he saw Thomas again. He said that he didn't think he was going to see Eddie anytime soon. Eddie's friend told him Eddie was leaving town to join Danielle. Art thought maybe the two were going to get back together.

The storm continued for two days and delayed my travel plans. I called in to the Algonquin and the Lafayette, but Thomas had not come back. Somehow, I knew that he was fine. I did not call Margery, although I thought hard about it. When they cleared the roads, I drove by Thomas's house. I did not go in when I saw that his car was not there. I went back to my apartment for the last time, packed my things, and drove home to Binghamton.

CHAPTER 22

Living back at home became uncomfortable after about five minutes. After a warm greeting, Barbara insisted that I sleep in the basement. The old spare bedroom had been turned into a nursery for their recent baby, and my old bedroom had been appropriated by Barbara for a "crafts room" that was off limits to anyone but her. It might have been a tolerable homecoming if I had an embarkation planned, but I had nothing definite ahead. Perhaps Barbara was thinking of this when I heard her suggest to my father that I should start paying rent after two days at home.

The whole Christmas–New Year's holiday time was pretty miserable. I smiled little and daydreamed often. Barbara and Dad generally ignored me, although much of that was probably my fault. I was still more focused on the events of the recent past than on my near-term future. My enthusiasm barely limped along during the week before the holiday, but on Christmas Eve I mustered the energy to called Margery.

"Margery, it's Julian. Merry Christmas."

"Julian, it's so good to hear your voice. How was your drive home?"

"Well, it was in December in upstate New York; that probably says it all."

"Was there very much snow?"

"Oh yes, very much snow. Did you hear from Thomas?"

"Yes, I did," she said. I held my breath before she continued. "He's fine. He hasn't come home yet, but he'll be here in time for church tomorrow morning. He hurt his arm working on some sheet metal on the hotel heating system. He said he slipped and he got a deep cut that a doctor had to stitch up. The doctor said it would heal fine, but Thomas had to stay for a follow-up check."

"How is he doing emotionally after the break-up with Danielle?" I asked.

"I think it was a big blow to him, but I've now talked with him a few times, and he seems stronger each day."

Then we talked about how she was getting along and about how my home situation was working out. Since I was talking in our living room, my conversation was not completely frank but sugar-coated in keeping with the season. She said she would have Thomas call me when she saw him the next day.

I waited until after New Year's Day to call again. In truth, I wasn't entirely sure that I wanted to speak with him. I still didn't want to think about that night in the storm. When I called, Margery answered.

"Hi, Margery, it's Julian."

"Hello, Julian. Did you have a nice Christmas?"

"Yes, it was great," I said. "How about yours?"

"Well, it was fine. Thomas came Christmas morning, and we went to church together. Then we exchanged gifts and had lunch together ..."

I sensed something missing. "But?"

"But he couldn't stay very long. He seemed fine, but he said he had to go back to deal with some issues. He left the farm right after lunch."

"I'm sorry it couldn't have been a longer visit," I said. "But you said he seemed good to you?"

"Oh yes, he seemed strong. Then he called me two days after he left and said that a friend from school invited him out to Colorado for the New Year's holiday. The hotel gave him some time off because of the arm injury. He asked if it was okay with me if he went."

"And?"

"Well, Julian, Thomas is a grown man. I'm not going to hold him back if he wants to go. Besides, I thought it might help him get his mind off the girl."

I hung up, promising that I'd call her again in a few days. She seemed to appreciate that.

I also called Art early in the new year. His card group had returned from their holiday travels, and at least for a few weeks, life seemed almost back to normal for him. I told him that Thomas had gone to Colorado for a while. Art said that he was relieved that Thomas seemed to have landed on his feet. I think Art had already put Thomas out of his mind and found himself a new handyman.

"Have you heard anything from Danielle?" I asked.

"No, nothing. But I found a new girl who is almost as pretty, and the customers like her a lot."

"What about Eddie?"

"Also nothing. I haven't seen him since that night, but I assume that wherever Danielle is, you'll find him there too. Good luck to both of them, I say."

I called Margery regularly in the early new year in search of news. I was ready to speak with Thomas by this time. I learned that he had such a great time out west that he wanted to travel a little longer. He was going south into Arizona and then to California. He did not expect to be back for several months. He did not have a fixed address but would check in with her frequently. She asked him to call me, but he never did. Time passed, and while I spoke to Margery frequently, I never heard from Thomas. She said he did travel to Arizona and then to California. He went to LA and then San Diego and then his money ran low. In San Diego, he took a job. He was working as a mechanic by day and played in a piano bar at night.

My life course was starting to firm up. I was accepted to graduate school and was able to arrange the loans to finance it. A future faculty member put me in touch with one of their alums, who offered me a job until my classes started in the fall. I worked for a newspaper in Buffalo for the next several months. I was not delighted with the geography, but the job was good for me. The winter weather in Buffalo stayed as brutally cruel as it started in Indiana. It was one of the coldest winters of the century.

I spoke with both Margery and Art at weekly intervals at that time. Margery continued to give positive reports on Thomas, and although he still never called me, I felt comforted by Margery's updates. Art kept me up with the happenings of the hotel, the Algonquin, and his card group. While he continued to expect letters or postcards from Danielle or Eddie, they never came.

"Something funny did come up a few days ago," he told me in one of our conversations. "Danielle's mother came in here about half drunk wondering if Danielle was owed any back pay. I bought her a drink, and she told me she had put Jenny on a plane to Phoenix a week ago. She couldn't remember Danielle's address though."

"Did she say anything about Eddie?" I asked.

"No, but she wouldn't. She never cared for him."

Art went on to say that Danielle's mother thought it was unlikely that Danielle would ever come back. Art sounded pleased as he described Danielle's situation. He took it as a positive that she had achieved her life's dream and escaped the town.

The winter continued with a fury. The snow had come, had only partially gone, and had come again. The snow was difficult, but the temperature was worse. The river in town stayed largely frozen until early March. Art called me on the day of the news.

"Julian, I just wanted to let you know they found Eddie today."

"Where was he?" I asked, nervous about what he was going to tell me.

"In the river, tangled in the roots of a willow tree."

I felt like my heart just dropped to my stomach. "I'm sorry," I said. I didn't know what else to say.

Art continued, "A couple of morning walkers saw his body in the river where the ice had cleared." He paused and then added, "It's tough on my sister."

"Yes, it must be."

My knees were feeling a bit weak, because I realized that I had been a witness to murder. But I think that in my heart I knew that already.

"What do they think happened?" I mumbled.

"The cops told my sister that when they pulled him out, they looked him over pretty closely. There was no sign of any foul play. It looks like an accident. They think he had too much to drink and walked too close to the bank. Remember, it was real snowy that night. Maybe he got careless."

"Yes, I remember," I said.

"Even though that's the theory, the police want to talk with you and Thomas to see if they can get any additional details of that night he was last seen."

Art gave me the number to contact the detective on the case. I called the detective. Yes, I told him, Eddie had been drinking that night, but that was not unusual. I told him my version of the story of how Eddie and Thomas were thrown out of the bar.

"Did you see either of them after they left?" the detective asked.

"No. I went right home. It was no night to hang around outside."

"I remember that storm," said the detective. "Have you talked with Thomas since that night?"

"No, I haven't," I said.

"The only odd thing about this case was that there was a knife scabbard on the body but no knife. Do you remember him taking the knife out at the bar?"

"No. I never saw him take out his knife."

"I wonder if he pulled the knife trying to hack out of the ice and never had the chance to put it back," said the detective almost to himself.

"What do you think happened?" I asked.

"This isn't the first time we've been called because of Eddie and his drinking. I just think he picked a bad night to get drunk and go for a walk near the river. I don't think it's much more complicated than that."

The detective seemed satisfied with our conversation, and I gave him my contact information if he wanted to speak with me further.

"If you speak with your friend, Thomas, make sure he gives me a call," said the detective before disconnecting the phone.

If the police checked the hospital emergency rooms for anything suspicious, I never heard about it, or perhaps Thomas had considered that and either paid cash with an assumed name or dealt with his wound outside of the usual local emergency rooms. I never found out.

About a month after they found Eddie, Margery gave me Thomas's new semipermanent mailing address in San Diego. It was a post office box, but it was an address. I wrote him four letters over the next month. I was just catching him up on my life since college and on my new life in Buffalo. I even apprised him of Margery's life as I followed it from our telephone calls.

A week after posting the last letter, I received a response. Thomas's long letter was newsy and, except for one bombshell, generally superficial. Thomas described his trip thus far and the jobs he had taken. He wrote about the climate, the people, and the ocean. He did not make any mention of Danielle, Jenny, or Eddie. At the end of the letter, he confided that he had given a great deal of thought about the direction in his life. He had made a decision he had not shared yet with Margery. I remember what he wrote:

I made the decision to enlist in the marines. It may surprise you, but I know this is the right thing for me. I have no doubt that I am meant to do this for myself and for everyone else in my life.

I assumed that during his preinduction physical exam he made no mention of "nervous problems" or any psychiatric care.

I heard nothing again from Thomas for six months, although I continued to grow closer to Margery. She and I continued to speak and write regularly, and through Margery, I was able to follow what he was doing. He completed his recruit training in San Diego and at Camp Pendleton. Margery went to his boot camp graduation ceremony and wrote me afterward:

Julian,

I attended Thomas's graduation ceremony from marine recruit training today. Thomas looked so handsome and strong in his uniform. He reminded me of James in so many ways. I'm so proud of him, although this was not the kind of graduation I expected for him. He has chosen a different path for his life than I ever would have imagined. But James would have been so proud to be standing there with me. I miss James more than ever.

I look forward to our next conversation. I'll ask Thomas to call you.
Fondly,

Margery

Thomas did not call for a month, and we had a few more conversations after that. We did not speak over the next year, but he wrote occasionally. He had undergone additional infantry training and was deployed to Vietnam. Margery was always worried, but she kept relying on her faith to keep him alive each day. She met Thomas once in Hawaii during that first year. After his first twelve months there, he came back to the states for a longer time. He went to Quantico for additional training but was able to come back to Indiana for a visit. I tried to arrange a time to come down to Virginia to visit, but our schedules never permitted it.

Over the telephone, Margery explained that Thomas was going to redeploy to Vietnam. I wrote to him, and for a time his correspondence would come about every six weeks. After a half dozen letters, though, they stopped arriving. I didn't dwell on it since I was then out of school and hustling stories for a few technical magazines. I was living in Washington, DC.

I did manage to visit Margery at the farm when I had to be in Chicago on business. Margery looked much older, and the farmhouse and outbuildings were all in need of repair. She was still warm and welcoming to me. She derived great support from her church and saw a few lady friends regularly. There were apparently several widows who helped one another in her congregation. Thomas explained to her in the last letter that it was difficult for him to write and that she should not assume that fewer correspondences meant anything other than that the logistics were complicated. Having her friends around helped her to deal with Thomas's absence.

When I explained to Margery that I had a new assignment that would cause me to travel to Vietnam, she was delighted at the prospect of the two of us seeing one another again. With concerted effort and with many letters and telephone calls, she was able to align our schedules to arrange for us to meet in Saigon.

After that first trip, I found my new contact "in-country," thanks to Thomas. Anna was a much better correspondent than Thomas had been. She, in fact, was more current with Thomas than Margery was. Anna was also the sole reason I continued to hector my editor for additional assignments to Vietnam.

After we met, Anna had continued to work with the children of war. Her clinic and hospital provided the acute treatment for the children's injuries. When the children were stable and ready to be moved, she worked with the orphanage Thomas and I had visited. The children would go to the orphanage for longer-term recovery and rehabilitation. Most of the children Thomas visited before had come from Anna's clinic.

Anna and I met in Saigon for dinner as soon as I arrived. We had our favorite quiet restaurant, and she was waiting there when I arrived. I still remember how good it felt to hold her again when we met.

"I missed you terribly," I said.

"I missed you too," she said. "How long can you stay this time?"

"Three or four days."

"Call it four," she said.

"Okay, four. How are the kids?"

"The clinic has been steady but there are some problems at the orphanage ..."

"What's wrong?"

"Mama Dao, the elderly woman who is the orphanage director, is very sick."

"What's she sick with?"

"It's cancer. It's pretty far advanced. The doctors think it's a stomach primary, but it's all through her liver now. She also has a lot of bone pain."

"That's a shame," I said.

"We've had to keep more of the kids at the clinic since some of the orphanage girls are tending Mama Dao in her village. They're very short-staffed now."

I sat and listened.

"Julian, Mama Dao's village is south along a small river near the Mekong. I want to say my final good-bye to her tomorrow. I really love that woman. Can you come with me? It would really mean a lot."

"Yes, sure."

"I heard that Thomas was going to try to get there if he can swing transportation."

"I'd love to see him," I said.

The trip to the delta area was slow even though we started out very early. It was often a dangerous and unstable trek with the fighting, but the problems this day were neither exotic nor heroic. There was a multi-vehicle accident that blocked the highway, and it took over an hour to clear it. Apparently some livestock had wandered onto the highway and the first car stopped short. His brakes jammed and he swerved into the oncoming traffic, creating the accident.

The trip took about four hours, and we were two hours later than we expected. When we reached the village, it took little time to find the old woman. She was well known both by her history and by her work. Her American friends were welcome. We made our way over to her modest single-room house.

The house was partially on stilts, with the front portion sitting supported over the river. The river beyond was alive with the traffic of the ubiquitous flat-bottom boats. Fruits, rice bags, chickens, pigs, and people were ferried along the river in both directions. The river's frenetic choreography contrasted markedly to the solemn tranquility within the small house.

The smell of burning incense filled the house, and several villagers were there to show respect. Two of the elders quietly chanted prayers around the peaceful woman who reclined in a bed in the corner of the large room. Anna waited for her turn to see the old woman. When she approached her bedside, the dying patient reached out for her giving a feeble smile.

Anna spoke to her slowly and tenderly in Vietnamese. I heard Anna repeat, "Mama Dao, Mama Dao," and then she lingered there, crying and holding the woman's hand. The old woman, with a karmic serenity, patted Anna's hand and then let it go. Anna understood and retreated so that others could come to the bedside.

Anna rejoined me, and we exited the small house. I put my arm around her as she tried to collect herself. Thomas was nowhere to be seen. However, as we started to walk away from the house, a US naval officer, a lieutenant, walked toward us on the path. His insignia identified him as a medical officer, and he was carrying a doctor's bag. Anna knew him, and they exchanged hellos. Anna then introduced me. The officer was a friend of Thomas's. He was a surgeon whose services the clinic was sometimes able to use for their children.

Anna inquired about Thomas.

"He was here about an hour ago," explained the doctor. "He said he couldn't stay long. He said that he was sorry he missed you but was going out on a limb by being here in the first place. He had to return to his duty station as quickly as possible."

Sensing our next question, he continued. "Anna, I'm only here because Thomas asked me to come to try to make your friend as medically comfortable as I could. I looked in on her back in Saigon as well. I'm doing this as a favor for Thomas."

Then he looked at us and said, "You know, he's a pretty amazing guy to have kept the orphanage going. I don't know where he gets the money. There's no one else who would have done it." Then the doctor looked into his bag, located the medication he needed, and walked into the house.

We made it back to Saigon before dark and had a good visit over the next few days. We never saw Thomas.

CHAPTER 23

I was staring out the window of our cabin's veranda watching the Ho Chi Minh City skyline when Anna returned. I had lost track of the time.

"Do you want to see my scarf now or should I surprise you tonight?" she asked.

I looked up and smiled at her. I think I had been through this drill a hundred times.

"I'd love to see it now," I said.

She smiled and put the scarf over her shoulders.

"It's very pretty," I said. "It looks great on you."

"Do you want to go to town now or stay on the ship and go in after lunch?" she asked.

"Let's go in about twenty minutes. We'll have to find a new favorite place, you know. Ho-Dacs is no more."

"Okay, let's do that. I'm going to run to the concierge for some suggestions. I'll be back in a little while."

She started to leave wearing her scarf.

"I thought you were saving the scarf for tonight."

She smiled. "No, I like it on. I'll wear it today. I'll see you in a little bit. You get ready to go." And then she left, and my thoughts drifted out the window again.

After I left Vietnam the last time, Anna continued to write me frequently. I could not wait for her to leave Vietnam so we could spend more time together. I felt selfish encouraging her to leave, but, well, I was selfish about her. She mentioned Thomas in her letters only to say that she had not seen him. He managed to courier cash to the orphanage, but he himself did not come back south. Mama Dao died a few days after I returned home, and Thomas did not make another trip to see her.

The telephone call came about two months after I returned to Washington. It was an unusual call since it came after eleven in the evening. After debating whether to answer, I picked up the receiver. The quavering voice on the other end was Margery's. We had only spoken two days earlier. I feared the worst.

"Julian, I'm sorry to call, but I have some bad news," she said.

I braced myself, but when she told me, it felt even more awful than I was expecting.

"They came by today and told me that Thomas had died." She said it quickly except for the last word, which stuck in her throat. She paused, and I could hear the crying through the line. "He died in action. They said he was a hero." She spoke with great difficulty.

There was long pause now as she was having trouble speaking. "They said he saved a lot of men."

"I'm so sorry, Margery. I'm so sorry. I'll come out on the first plane tomorrow."

"No, Julian. I don't want that. I want to be by myself for a little while."

"Of course," I said.

"I want to get off the telephone now. It's been a long day, but we'll talk tomorrow. I'm going to bury him in Arlington. They said he was eligible, and I think that's where he should be."

"Sure," I said. "I'll call you in the morning."

"Okay. Good night."

I replaced the phone. I was numb. A giant knot grew inside of me, and then I started to cry. I cried for an hour, confused as to whom or what I was crying for. Thomas seemed to want this. He had any number of opportunities to leave and have someone else stand in his place. He might have done his job less aggressively and perhaps not have attracted as much attention. I don't know why I cried. I was partially angry with Thomas for bringing this upon himself. I was angry at the country for being in Vietnam. And I was angry at the world for relying on Americans my age to keep the order. I cried for Thomas. I cried for Danielle and her baby, and I even cried for Eddie. I cried for Thomas's father and sister. I cried for my mother and Margery and myself. I cried about being alive and about not being alive. I cried for loss of youth, and innocence, and friendship.

Margery and I talked daily until the funeral. She had a good network of support from her church and sounded stronger each day, although I know that was wishful thinking on my part. The funeral would be in a few weeks, and Margery wanted to make sure I was going to be in town. I told her to make the arrangements and that whenever it was, I would be there.

I wrote to Anna about what happened. I did not know whether she knew, and I could not reach her on the telephone. Margery seemed to be dealing with this as well as anyone could ask. The marines made all the burial arrangements for her. It was to be a burial with military honors but as per her wishes would be confined to a gravesite service. Margery's friends from Indiana wanted to stand with her during the burial, but she insisted that they not spend the time or the money to travel to Washington. She would come alone. Thomas's other friends and the university would be told after the fact, since she didn't want the fuss or the remembrances of Thomas's earlier problems.

On the day of the burial, I met Margery at Washington National Airport. She was going to fly in and fly back to Chicago that same day. I met her coming out of her gate and gave her a hug. She was dressed in black and seemed to be practicing the toughness needed to face the day.

We had ample time before the late-morning service, and I didn't want to spend it all walking in Arlington. I drove her around Washington, since she told me it had been over twenty years since she had been back to the capital. The weather was unseasonably warm for early October, and it was quite pleasant. The Capitol Building stood out against a perfect blue sky, and the usual traffic had thinned to some degree by midmorning. Driving past the White House, we saw the now-constant gaggle of war protesters and their placards on the sidewalks. The sign reading "Baby Killers" was the most prominent.

Margery looked past the crowd and commented quietly. "The White House looks so impressive. I had forgotten. It's been years since I've been in this town. It makes you proud to be an American."

I smiled at her as I drove.

We drove back to the Mall around the Lincoln Memorial and then over the Arlington Bridge. We both looked toward the Iwo Jima Memorial and then entered the cemetery.

After locating the administration building, I followed Margery to the appropriate office, where she was asked to sign some papers. The navy chaplain who would conduct the service was called, and he joined us in the office. He offered to drive us to the gravesite, but since we had our own car, we agreed to meet him there.

We followed his directions to the proper section, going between rows and rows of white marble headstones. Margery said almost nothing and relied on me to lead her. When we came to the site, the grave had been prepared, and the officer in charge of the funeral made his way over to us and introduced himself. He stayed close to

Margery and conveyed a confidence that he would get her though this. There must have been three hundred marines, soldiers, sailors, and civilians gathered for the service. Many senior officers were among them.

At the scheduled time, the hearse pulled up to the section. The command "present arms" was given, and the marines saluted and the rifle team presented arms. The casket team of six pallbearers secured the casket from the hearse and followed the chaplain to the gravesite. A senior enlisted man adjusted the flag over Thomas's casket and then stepped away.

The chaplain was brief but talked about Thomas's great sense of duty and love for his fellow marines. The line that I remembered most was "Had it not been for the selfless honor and heroic sacrifice of this one marine, thirty marines would be dead today." Then he said a prayer.

There was no mention of the many kids Thomas took care of or the other lives he had saved in Vietnam. The rifle team then initiated a volley, and a single bugler played "Taps."

Margery held up well until the playing of "Taps" but then dissolved into tears on my shoulder. Her sobs sounded even louder after the music stopped as two of the pallbearers precisely folded the flag. Then in the time-honored tradition set by tens of thousands of American dead, the flag was passed to the noncommissioned officer in charge and then to the officer in charge. The OIC presented the flag to the navy chaplain, who walked it to Margery. She was only slightly more composed by this time. She clutched the flag momentarily and then handed it to me to hold for her.

Most of the assembled marines filed by the casket in respect. Several of these heroes wept openly and uncontrollably. Then Thomas was lowered in the ground, and that was it. A few of the marines stopped to speak with Margery. I took a step back, particularly when two senior officers spent time telling Margery about her son's heroism and love for his comrades.

I was holding the flag, and a senior enlisted marine, a gunnery sergeant, came over to me.

I greeted him, and he smiled at me.

"Did you serve with Thomas, Gunny?"

"Yes, we served together. He was one of the finest men I've ever had the pleasure to serve with."

"How was it at the end?"

"I wasn't there, but I heard this from guys who were. He had just started out on one of his three-day patrols. He often worked alone. He didn't even want a spotter. The guys knew he was out there. A platoon left on patrol about two hours after he left, and a few hours later, they were in it deep. It was open country with some high ground around. NVA had them on all sides. The NVA was at least at company strength, maybe two. They were closing in, and it was pretty sticky. Air support was not coming, and it didn't look too good for our team. Then suddenly Charlie starts falling dead in his tracks. Thomas was up on the high ground, and he had a good look at the battlefield. He clipped about fifteen of them before they started dropping back. He killed another ten or so in retreat. The platoon was able to pull out when the NVA turned their attention to Thomas. He kept them busy while the rest of the guys got away."

The marine started to choke up and paused to compose himself.

"We went back and found him the next day. There were another twenty dead NVA in his general area; a few more nearby him were killed with knife wounds. He had run out of ammunition. He was hit a few times before a head shot took him out. He saved a lot of guys." The gunny paused again. "He was a marine's marine."

"Did he ever talk about home to you?" I asked.

The gunny brightened, "Oh, yeah. All the time."

"What did he talk about?"

"I guess he grew up on a farm he always wanted to go back to. He seemed to love that place. He also had this girl who wanted to marry him after he got back. He talked about her a lot."

"What was her name?" I asked.

He thought a moment. "I don't know if he ever said."

I glanced back briefly at Margery to make sure she was all right and then asked, "Did he ever talk about playing the piano?"

"No, was he any good?"

"Yes. He was pretty good."

"No kidding. He never mentioned it." The marine seemed surprised by this.

"Did he ever tell you he played football?"

"No. He didn't talk about it. Did he play in high school before coming in the Corps?"

"Yes," I said. "He was a pretty good player."

The marine nodded. "He did a lot of things well."

I agreed.

The gunny patted me on the arm and walked off.

I rejoined Margery. A pregnant woman about my age came up to her. She had been crying. Her husband was a marine lieutenant, and he was in command of the platoon Thomas had saved. The young wife wanted to convey her husband's gratitude for Thomas's sacrifice.

Margery smiled and told the woman "Thank you" and gave her a hug, telling her how much it meant to her that she came.

The Arlington staff provided a woman to help us out of there and to deal with any other details. Thomas's personal effects, medals and commendations, and paperwork would be sent directly to the farm. The Arlington lady asked if Margery wanted to ship Thomas's flag.

Margery did not. She also refused the flag case the cemetery provided. I think she wanted the flag carried openly for everyone to see it and to understand what it meant.

The drive back was in the sparse midday traffic, and it was a short trip to National Airport. We had plenty of time before her flight.

"Would you like to go somewhere for lunch?" I asked her.

"No, thank you, Julian. I'm not hungry now."

"Is there anywhere you'd like to go? We have a lot of time."

"No. Let's just go to the airport. I'm very tired."

When we arrived at National, she wanted me to park the car and come into the terminal with her. She didn't want me to drop her off; she wanted to stay with me.

I parked, and we went into the terminal. We found a quiet sitting area and I checked on her flight while she waited. I brought her a cold drink, which she put on the table untouched. I was still carrying the flag for her.

We sat for several minutes until she broke the silence.

"Will you still check up on me every week?" she asked.

"Yes, Margery, I will."

"Good," she said. "And will you come by the farm whenever you get back to the college or come to Chicago?"

"I certainly will."

"And if you are free for Thanksgiving, will you bring Anna by and spend it with me?"

"There's no place I'd rather be."

"Thank you." Then she started to cry again, her strength drained away. The tears came heavy. "You know I'm all alone now," she managed to say through her sobs.

I nodded and put my arm around her while she cried. "You're not alone, Margery," I said. "I'll always be here for you."

She sobbed for some time before she spoke again.

"He was a good son."

"Yes, he was," I agreed. "He did a lot of good over there, Margery. He saved a lot of men. Anna told me he helped many, many children."

"I know," she said. "He told me about it. He was a good man."

We waited a few minutes quietly; neither of us spoke. Then she checked her wristwatch and patted me on the hand.

She placed her trembling brown hand over the blue-and-white starred folded flag triangle in my arms. She let her hand linger there as if afraid that holding it would confirm the terrible reality of the day. Eventually, she gripped it and drew it tightly to her chest. Then she held it like she would never let it go.

"Julian," she said.

"Yes, Margery?" I answered.

I looked closely at her. There was a distant look in her eyes. I imagined she was looking ahead to her life without Thomas or grandchildren or any of the other dreams she had held.

"It's going to be all right," she said calmly.

I tried to muster a weak smile in response. She sat without speaking for long time. I think she was praying, and I prayed too. I prayed that someday I could understand how much of this was God's will and how much of it was the randomness of life.

Between my prayers, I thought of the incredible talents Thomas had had and the demons he had conquered. Ernie might have said, "In the words of the philosopher, 'Heroism is an obedience to a secret impulse of an individual's character.'" I could not imagine the depths of the secrets in Thomas's character.

After a time, Margery reached over and squeezed my hand. I looked up.

"You can go now," she said.

I slowly turned my head and looked into her eyes.

"It's all right. You go ahead now," she said firmly, and I knew she meant it.

Then I hugged her like my dying mother. I hugged her long enough for my fresh tears to drop on her shoulder. When we broke the hug, our eyes locked and we both realized there was nothing more to be said. I kissed her on the cheek and walked to my car. I knew I would see her again soon.

I watched the Ho Chi Minh City skyline, waiting for Anna to return. I wept softly, thinking about it all again.

When Anna came in I dried my face, but she knew.

She gave me a tender smile.

"Not only is today the anniversary of Margery's death, but it's the tenth anniversary. Did you remember that?" she asked.

I returned her smile. "Yes, I remembered," I said. "I remember it all like yesterday."

The End

ACKNOWLEDGMENTS

All quotations from the "preacher" are more precisely identified as from the letters of St. Paul. All quotations attributed to the "poet" are lines from Walt Whitman. All quotations ascribed to the "philosopher" are the wise words of Ralph Waldo Emerson.

SPECIAL THANKS

I would like to thank family and friends who provided thoughtful input to this book in its various iterations. Thank you, Emily, Peter, John, Lee Anne, Alex, and especially Cissy. Thanks also to Ellen Epps, Lucia Dorsey, and Melissa Starr for your insightful and critical editorial input.

ABOUT THE AUTHOR

William Claypool attended the University of Notre Dame and has taught at the University of Illinois at Chicago, the University of Pittsburgh, and the University of Pennsylvania. He lives outside of Philadelphia with his wife and their dogs. During segments of his life, he was a football player, a naval medical officer, and a night bellman.